The Playboy's Secret Virgin

TASHA FAWKES

M.S. PARKER

ISBN: 978-1-941837-45-0
ISBN-10: 1-941837-45-X

tashafawkes.com

CONTENTS

CHAPTER ONE
JANE

Taxi!"

I tuck a long strand of chestnut brown hair behind my ear with one hand as I fight to flag down a cab with the other. Just my luck that there aren't any Ubers available when I decided to splurge on a ride to my new job so I won't arrive all flushed. I wave my arms to get the attention of one of the many passing cabs, but it's no use. After only a few months in the city, I haven't yet learned the art of making a cabbie notice me.

"I guess it's the subway," I mutter to myself and try not to curse. There's still plenty of time. I'll even get there early.

Nothing can get me down today. Sure, it's Monday, and the faces of the people I pass on the way to the station reflect their total lack of excitement over starting another week. But I'm not starting just another week. I feel like announcing to everybody that this is my first day of work at a job that isn't retail. Maybe they'll wish me luck. Then I catch the eye of a lady with a stroller, and she shoots me a dirty look before hurrying off. Okay. Maybe I shouldn't bother.

My first day working at one of the fastest growing ad agencies in Manhattan. I still can't believe my luck. I only went to the job fair because I had nothing to lose. I was hardly making anything in my first job out of college, and to say I was bored working as a mail room clerk would be a drastic understatement. I figured since I had good grades in school and a decent resumé—an advertising major, strong references, knowledge of graphic arts, expertise with design programs like Photoshop—that I had a pretty good shot, and I was right. The HR representative from James Enterprises called three days later to offer me the position as assistant to Anthony James, the son of the founder.

Anthony James. I'm sure panties dissolve at the mention of his name all the time. I've heard a thing or two about him, but nothing concrete. He's sort of a bad boy, but aren't most rich kids who never have to work for a thing in their lives? They grow up too fast and get into trouble. I guess that's his story, but I don't exactly pay attention to the social pages. I have better things to do than follow a rich boy's antics.

Still, I can't walk into the job with any preconceived notions of who he is. I have a bad habit of doing that, letting my imagination spin out of control, and generally in the worst way possible. One of my foster moms used to tell me I'd have an ulcer before I turn twenty-five. Four more years to go before that happens but have my fingers crossed that she'll be wrong.

I'm not letting myself down that road with my new boss. I'll give him a chance so long as he's signing my checks. I've never had a job that pays as much as this one—my last job barely paid enough for me to afford my shoebox of an apartment. Then again, that's the way life goes in New York. Pay through the nose for a closet-sized apartment and just be grateful for the chance to live in one of the biggest, most incredible cities in the world.

I sigh as I step onto the subway car and immediately pitch forward when a big, burly guy in a Mets sweatshirt slams into me from behind. No apology, no anything. Go figure. I grab onto one of the metal poles and fix my gaze somewhere off in the distance, the way everybody does when they're on the subway. Don't look directly at anybody, just sort of gaze out at nothing. Eye contact might be misconstrued as an invitation to chat, and this isn't like back home where most people already know everyone else and it's rude to not want to have a three-hour conversation about the weather. Talk to the wrong person here and it can lead to trouble.

Big city life has many rules to remember, and I still have trouble keeping it all straight even after living here for almost eight months. Manhattan is not far away from where I grew up in rural northeastern Pennsylvania. Less than two hours by car, but it might as well be the other side of the planet. Maybe on another planet entirely.

The frantic energy, the honking horns, the constant

activity like bees in a hive. The people, everywhere, packing the streets and sidewalks. And the way they somehow manage to ignore everybody else around them! The first time I saw a group of people crossing the street on a red light without even looking to see if cars were coming, I screamed. The craziest part? Nobody looked around to see what I was screaming about.

I'm okay with the noise, at least. That's one thing I had to get used to at an early age, living with up to four or five other foster kids at a time. I'm already a pro at ignoring noise filtering through thin walls, so living in a crowded apartment building and hearing everybody else's business is no big deal.

Neither is living in a small space. I never had a bedroom of my own until I moved out of the college dorm—my entire life, I've had to share. Living in a shoebox is actually a step up. So what if the bathroom is really just a tiny walled-off section of the apartment, which is really just a single room with a sink and small stove? I learned early on that "studio apartment" means "we took a single room and now pretend a person can live there comfortably." I've also learned how much food I can fit in a very tiny fridge.

I catch sight of my reflection in one of the grimy train windows. The waves I took so long to curl this morning are still looking good, spilling over my shoulders and onto my chest. I'm wearing a long black Chanel coat I could never have afforded anywhere other than at the consignment shop where I found it. The gray suit and light pink blouse are new—I don't know how the office runs, what the dress code is, but there's no way to go wrong in a suit. I can always dress down if I need to. Besides, the pink brings out color in my cheeks and makes my gray eyes sparkle. I figure I can use all the help I can get to make Anthony like me.

Speaking of people liking me, Mr. Mets Sweatshirt is nudging me a little more than he needs to be. We're not even shaking back and forth, yet he keeps making contact. I let it go for a stop or two, but when he flat-out rubs up against me, I turn to him.

"Can I help you with something?" I ask in a clear, loud voice, looking him straight in the eye.

He shrinks back, cheeks staining red. "No."

"It's just that you seem to be having trouble keeping your balance."

"No, I'm good." He looks down at the floor. I roll my eyes and go back to staring out the window. That's the thing about most creeps. Once you stare them down, they back off.

I suppose growing up where I did have its advantages when it comes to dealing with creeps.

The train lurches to a stop at my station, and I manage to elbow my way out the door and hurry up to the sidewalk. After a quick look around to orient myself, I head over to the nearest Starbucks. *A little kissing up never hurt anybody*, I tell myself as I wait in line. What does he like, this Anthony James? I try to picture him in my head, based on the few pictures I remember seeing. Tall, with a strong-featured face. Square jaw, deep-set blue eyes, dark hair wore swept back from his forehead. I saw him once in a picture from a cycling race, and he had a body to kill for. Broad shoulders and long, muscular legs. He'd be at home on a billboard advertising underwear. I'd look at that billboard. I'd stare at it all day.

Shut it down. I shake my head to clear my thoughts. The last thing I need to do is get all googly-eyed over my boss. I won't be that pathetic.

"I'll have a venti non-fat mocha…an iced venti soy latte..." I rattle off the names of four drinks, four being the most I can feasibly carry in one of those cardboard carrier things. Eight-thirty. Thirty minutes until I have to report to the office, and it's only a block away. Things are looking good.

Until I wait twenty minutes for my drinks. I didn't take that into consideration before stopping in. I nearly run the rest of the way to the office in my brand-new shoes, and I can just about hear blisters popping up on my feet along the way. Between that and the way I zigzag through other pedestrians—why *are there so many?*—I'm a total flustered mess by the time I reach the tall glass doors of the building James Enterprises calls home.

I can't get my ID card to work when I swipe it over the sensor by the door no matter how many times I try. There's no way to get inside.

Unbelievable. I try to catch the eye of the receptionist, sitting behind a desk along the marble wall. Just my luck there isn't anybody coming in or out while I'm standing there feeling like the world's biggest idiot.

When she sees me, she buzzes me in. I open the heavy door and hurry through the lobby with a sheepish grin. "Thank you," I breathe. "You're a lifesaver. It's my first day working for Mr. James, and I don't want to be late."

Instead of smiling back, the way a civilized person would do, she rolls her eyes. "Oh. Another one."

Another one? What's that mean? I almost want to ask, but bite my tongue and keep my eyes on the floor the rest of the way to the elevator instead. So much for a friendly welcome on my first day. It shouldn't surprise me, though. I've never had a warm welcome anywhere.

But I've never given up before, and I'm not going to start now.

I muffle a curse as someone else jostles me. I need to remember that people aren't always friendly in the city, and what better way to remember than by fighting my way onto the elevator? There has to be three dozen people trying to squeeze their way onto one car, but since I'm near the front I manage to secure a spot. Then, I get squished as everybody squeezes on behind me.

"Oh, no," I whisper, horrified, as I realize I feel wetness running down the front of my brand-new blouse. I look down to confirm that I'm spilling coffee all over myself. My blouse is now nearly see-through—I can just about make out the lace of my bra. My cheeks burn hotter than the surface of the sun. What a great first impression, and all I wanted to do was make my boss smile on the first day. Instead, I'll always be the girl who walked in on her first day with coffee all over her shirt.

I'm alone by the time I reach the top floor, and so miserable I could cry. The inside of the elevator doors are shiny enough to let me see my rumpled, stained self in the reflection. *It couldn't get worse than this.*

Or so I think until the elevator doors open, and I find myself standing face-to-face with none other than Anthony James himself, and I see that yes, things can get worse. Especially when I realize the photographers who took the photos I've seen should lose their jobs. Anthony James is the most gorgeous man I've ever seen in person...and he's looking me up and down with an expression of boredom and disgust.

Great first impression, Jane.

CHAPTER TWO
ANTHONY

It's not even lunch time yet and already I'm bored to death. Different day, same story.

My whole fucking life.

I sit behind my desk pushing papers around, trying to muster up the desire to do something. Anything. Anything that will get my father off my back and make him believe I won't have a negative impact on his wonderful political campaign. I wish it were as easy as looking good—never a problem for me—and showing up at the office. It isn't. Why would it be? When has he ever given me a break?

I know, I know, listen to the poor little rich boy. When in my twenty-eight years has my life ever been difficult?

I stand up and go out to the empty desk that will soon seat my assistant. I roll my eyes just thinking about the charity case Dad's saddling me with. An intern, technically, since he isn't sure yet that I won't completely fuck things up. It's all just another part of the image he wants me to fulfill. Successful businessman, in love with the family business, nose up his father's ass. The perfect son. Totally rehabilitated from his bad boy, whoring ways.

It's all such a joke, but nobody's laughing. Least of all me.

It's not just the job that needs to change, either. No more late nights out on the town. No more clubbing. No more photos of me shit faced in the newspapers or tabloids, which is usually where I end up. My dad even hired me a driver, just in case I have a small drink and wanted to get behind the wheel. Anything that could affect his chances of getting elected. Forget about wanting me to be safe. I'm what I've always been to him. A means to an end.

He might as well take my balls while he's at it. I can't remember all the times I've told him to get himself a new son if I'm not good enough. Going all the way back to when I was a kid, I could never understand why he always found something wrong with me.

I notice the nods and smiles from the various female employees as I walk past their desks and open office doors and it just pisses me off even more. Another one of my father's new rules: lay off the women, or at least have the decency be discreet. And absolutely nothing inside the company. Like I would ever do that? I've never had any issues with the women working here. Not once.

I swear, the old man comes up with new rules every day. It's like he sits up all night pondering on how to ruin my life the fastest way.

Naomi gives me one of her "come hither" smiles as I approach the reception desk. I tell myself to ignore it, along with the way she's wearing her sweater dress. Not worth the headache, no matter how nice her tits are.

"Have you seen my father walk past yet this morning?"

She nods. "Oh, of course. He went straight to his office."

Of course.

I can't look at her anymore without giving in to the urge to ask her out for a drink just to spite my father, so I turn away in time for the elevator doors to open on an interesting sight: a girl with coffee soaking the front of her shirt. She's a stranger, too, and staring at me with a horrified expression, which tells me she's probably my new assistant. Only I would get that lucky.

I shake my head at her. I have no words. Then I go straight to my father's office, determined to tell him that faking my way through a job I hate is one thing, but saddling me with the mousey little thing in the elevator is something else.

Marta sees me coming and holds up a hand to stop me at her desk, just in front of the tall double doors leading to the inner sanctum. "He's in a meeting," she says with a shrug.

"Good thing, since I really came here to talk with you." I place both hands on the edge of the desk and lean in. "When are you going to stop this game you're play with me? You know we belong together."

She fans herself while rolling her eyes. "Stop. You're too much."

"I want to marry you and take you away from all this, Marta. Don't you know I've been saving myself for you all these years you've been working for Dad?" I give her my best sultry smile.

"Oh, now I know you're pulling my leg." She draws back with a smirk and pats her silver-streaked hair. "You haven't saved yourself for a minute."

I put my hands over my heart. "Those women didn't mean anything to me. I had to console myself during those long, lonely nights without you."

She shakes her head, and I decide to drop the banter. The truth is, even though we have our little jokes and I swear she's the only one for me, she's the closest thing I've had to a mother since my own died when I was two. Dad's the disciplinarian, while Marta doles out advice and gently lets me know when I'm being an idiot. She's the only person who can get away with it.

"Isn't your new assistant starting today?" she asks in a knowing tone of voice.

"Yeah. Let's not talk about her, okay?" Marta knows how I feel. She ought to, anyway, since Dad and I weren't quiet when we argued about it. "What time is his meeting scheduled to end?"

She scrolls through a schedule on her laptop. "There's no scheduled end time. Conference call with the CFO and his team. Who knows how long it'll take?"

"Great." Not like I have anything better to do, but I'd rather eat my own face than go back to my office and deal with coffee girl. Not the sort of mood I'm in.

My phone's in my back pocket, and I pull it out when it buzzes. It's my best friend, Tyler Gaines, and he's been needier than usual lately after breaking up with his girlfriend. He pretends he doesn't care and he's only texting because he's bored, but I know it's either text me or text the ex. I'd rather be the one, if only so he'll save face. Besides, she's a real bitch.

It's five o'clock somewhere. Let's blow off work and go out.

I shoot him a quick text back. *It's still morning. Are you serious?*

He replies immediately. *Hell yes. I'll go either way. Thought you'd be up for some fun.*

Am I up for some fun? Of course, especially since Dad's had me on a short leash. I'm sick of pretending to be a good guy. I'm even sicker of pretending to follow his rules when it never means getting his approval.

What will he think? I glance at his office doors and imagine how he'll flip the hell out when he finds out I left, and to go out with Tyler on top of that. He needs to remember that I'm not some underling he can order around. And I'm not a child anymore, no matter how much he tries to treat me like one.

"You know what, beautiful? Forget about it. I'll catch him later." I drop Marta a wink and a smile before turning around and heading straight for the elevator. Screw Dad and his rules and his election. I'm my own man, and it's time he realizes that.

CHAPTER THREE
JANE

When Anthony James walks away with a disgusted expression on his face, I hate myself just a little more. *Pretty impressive all right*, I think with a sinking heart. Could this day get any worse?

The receptionist here looks sympathetic. "You must be Jane."

"Guilty." I manage to smile. At least she seems nicer than the woman downstairs.

"Let me show you where you can put those." She pushes back from her desk and leads me down a short hallway to the kitchen, where I ditch the coffee carrier.

"Thanks," I say quietly. I have myself under control now, but it's a close thing.

"The employee restroom is two doors down on the right." She points. She takes a step, then hesitates before adding, "Don't let it ruin your day. That could happen to anyone."

Sure it could. I smile and thank her before heading for the restroom in attempt to make myself at least semi-presentable. Of course, I'm not a miracle worker, so there's only so much I can do. The blouse is a total wash. I'll be lucky if I don't get cited for indecent exposure thanks to the now see-through fabric.

While I'm standing in front of the automatic hand dryer and holding the blouse out to dry after washing it, a tall, leggy blonde walks in. The kind you hate on principle. Instead of pretending not to see me and hurrying to a stall like most women would, she leans against the sink, giving me a wry smile.

"You're the new girl, huh?"

I sigh. "Am I wearing a sign? Did somebody slap it on me in the elevator when I was busy making a mess of myself?"

I try to sound upbeat, but I'm too heart sore for that. I can't forget the look of disgust on Anthony's handsome face. All the hope I have for this job and what it means to my future is fading fast. I try to hold on to it, but I'm not sure I can, not when things are starting off so badly. Having spilled the coffee on Anthony is the only way things could have been worse.

"Think of it this way: the day can only get better from here. Right?" She smiles warmly. "I'm Chloe. Administrative assistant to the head of HR for the past ten months. I saw you come in here and thought you could use a friend."

She's completely disarming and seems genuine. For the first time since reaching the building, I relax enough to be able to breathe. My past tells me that I should be wary, but something about her makes me trust her to be as nice as she appears.

"I'm Jane Ward. Anthony James' new assistant."

"Uh-hmm." Her dark eyes go wide.

That's all she says, and I don't particularly feel like asking her to elaborate. I wish I never had to see him again, and he probably feels the same about me. Maybe I can convince someone to transfer me. I would be willing to take the mail room here.

"Come on." She checks herself out in the mirror above the sink. She's beautiful and clearly confident in who she is; the type of person I've always wanted to be.

Confident and secure of herself.

The closest I can come to that is pretending that I know what I'm doing, and as this morning proved, that never works.

"I'll show you around before taking you to your desk," she says as she gestures toward a stall.

I quickly step inside, pull off my jacket, and put back on the shirt. My bra is still a bit damp, but I'm hoping the stain will come out. Those things are expensive, and I'm a little too curvy to go without. I button up my jacket to hide most of the stain and then follow Chloe out the door.

The first day at a new job is always a blur. I'm sure I'll never learn everybody's name, but I'll do my best to try. I'll never remember the layout of the floor, either. So many faces, so many turns through the maze of cubicles and glass-walled conference rooms. It's a beautiful place, for sure, with high ceilings and plenty of windows letting natural light pour in. Even as my nerves knot in the pit of my stomach, I know I want to work here.

When the tour ends, we're standing next to an empty desk. "Well, I guess this is you," Chloe says, and I notice the way she runs a hand over her hair. Like she's fixing it.

Then I realize what she said. My desk. That means Anthony James' office is behind the dark wooden door. He could come out at any moment and give me that disgusted look again. Tell me to go home because he needs someone far more presentable than me. I have to sit or else risk falling over on my shaky legs.

"Here's your computer and all that jazz. Your login info is probably on a sticky note in the top drawer because nobody around here has any imagination or respect for security. I've gotta get back to my desk, but I'm sure I'll see you around."

Before I get a chance to thank her, she's gone, racing down the hall on mile-high heels.

I do what I used to do whenever I was put in a new home—never more than three years in one place—I allow myself thirty seconds of fear before pushing it down.

Okay. Time to learn the ropes and prove I'm not just some idiot bumpkin with a coffee fetish. Chloe was right about the info for my computer being in the top desk drawer, so I log in and go through my inbox. Lots of welcome messages, and a single request to visit the CEO, Anthony James' father, later this afternoon.

Shit.

My mouth feels dry all of a sudden. He wants to

meet me face-to-face? How many employees get that special honor? I have the feeling he wants to look me over to be sure I'm right as the assistant for his son. Here's hoping he's a little more forgiving than his off-spring, or at least more understanding of accidents.

It's time for my meeting with Mr. James, and I still haven't seen Anthony since the disaster this morning. It's a relief, for sure, but I feel like I've wasted the day. It didn't take me long to check my email and read every single page of the employee handbook. After that, there wasn't much to do. What's the point of sitting at my desk, wondering what's expected of me? I could do that at home.

An older, extremely sophisticated woman who reminds me of Meryl Streep sits outside the big guy's office. "You must be Jane. It's nice to meet you. If you would follow me?"

I'm sure she notices the still-visible stains on my shirt, but she has enough class to pretend she doesn't.

She leads me into Mr. James' office and I try not to gawk. The walls on two sides are entirely made of glass providing a breathtaking view of the city. Mr. James sits at a massive desk with his back to the windows. He's tall, handsome, with a mile-wide smile and perfect salt-and-pepper hair. He'd make a great anchorman for a news show.

"How's my son been treating you today?" he asks after a firm handshake. I feel his eyes travel over me, taking inventory. I must pass muster, even though he looks somewhat bemused by the stain that's still visible. I keep my head high and remind myself to exude confidence, even if I'm not feeling it.

"I haven't spoken to him yet, actually." Even though I keep my voice light, his expression darkens. Shit. Maybe I shouldn't be honest, but I've never been a good liar.

"And why is that?"

When I shake my head, his voice gets louder as he says, "Marta? Where's my son?"

"He took a client to dinner," she calls back.

I suddenly feel impossibly awkward as tension fills the air. Mr. James isn't happy. Not even a little. His mask slips slightly, and I see the man underneath: one seriously pissed-off father. If what Marta says is a lie, she delivers it smoothly, but Mr. James sees right through it, making me believe this isn't the first time she's offered it.

He walks me out of the office, and I wonder if he really wanted to meet me or if he only wanted to get dirt on his son. What could I possibly tell him after one day that he wouldn't already know? He shakes my hand again, then turns to Marta.

"Please let Anthony know that I expect him in the office bright and early tomorrow morning. Otherwise, there'll be hell to pay." With that, he turns on his heel, marches back inside, and closes the door.

I can feel my cheeks flushing as I look at Marta for some clue on how to react to this. She only shakes her head. "It's a father/son thing. I wouldn't worry too much about it."

Sure. No problem.

***

It's a pleasure to slide out of my heels the second I get home. My next priority is taking off my blouse and throwing it in the trash. Stupid blouse. Stupid me for thinking that I could make anything other than a mediocre impression. My lot in life isn't to be exceptional, but rather fade into the background. I hang up what's left of my suit and put on sweats and a tee. There's nothing like the joy of putting on comfy clothes after a day at the office. I can at least have the simple pleasures in life.

I curl up on the futon and am ready to nurse my first day sorrows with a bottle of wine and trashy TV when there's a knock at the door. I frown. Nobody ever knocks at my door. Ever.

I get up and glance around to see if anything in here can be used as a weapon.

"Who is it?" A girl doesn't just open the door on a stranger. Not even a country transplant like me would do that.

"Chloe."

Chloe? I mouth, suddenly ashamed of my poorly-furnished shoebox of an apartment. I'm sure she lives in a beautiful loft apartment somewhere with charm and character and all sorts of other buzz words that translate into high rent. She's probably standing out there, already regretting being in this neighborhood. Sure, it's not the worst, but it's far from New York City's best.

I figure I have nothing to lose by answering the door, so I do. If we're going to be friends, which maybe we are, she'll eventually find out how I live and where I come from.

She's still wearing her work clothes, and she still looks fantastic. Meanwhile, I'm wearing a t-shirt which is basically a series of holes with strips of fabric here and there. Only slightly more embarrassing than my coffee-stained blouse.

"Why are you here? Don't tell me you live in this building." My joke falls flat.

She smiles. "I wanted to take you out for a drink after work, but you bolted out too fast for me to catch you."

Yes, because I wanted to get the hell out and pretend the whole messy day never happened.

But I'm not rude.

"Do you want to come in?" She nods, and I step aside, however reluctantly.

"This is cute!" she exclaims as she looks around. "You're so creative, making such great use of your space."

That's probably the nicest way I've ever heard someone describe something this small. When I first saw it, for once I was grateful that my childhood had left me with very little in the way of possessions.

"How did you know where I live?" I motion to the futon where she manages to perch delicately without looking snotty about it.

She shrugs. "It's in your personnel file."

My jaw drops. "You looked at my file?"

"Yeah. Why not?" She shrugs again. "Anyway, I figured you need a drink after this morning. More than one drink, maybe."

I laugh and try not to let her see how nervous the suggestion makes me. "I'm pretty tired, to be honest. And I'm not much of a social butterfly. I go to bed early, too. I'm basically the cover of a AARP magazine."

Her laugh is rich and throaty. The sort of thing men would want to listen to for hours on end. "Come on, Jane. It's still early. Happy Hour is barely even over yet. One or two drinks won't keep you out too late. We can get something to eat, too. I promise, I won't keep you out too far past your bedtime, Grandma."

I have the feeling she's going to be a bad influence on me, but maybe a bad influence is just what I need. And it's not like I have many friends to fall back on. Maybe I could use a work friend, someone to go with the new start I hope to make.

"Okay. Give me a quick sec to get dressed."

"No," she says as she gives me a once over. "The homeless look is super in right now."

Chloe manages a straight face for about three seconds before bursting into laughter, and this time, I join her.

CHAPTER FOUR
ANTHONY

Dad's gonna kill me.

I can't help but think that with a wry smile as I lift a glass of Scotch to my lips. I've been thinking it all night, in club after club, every time I walk in and get recognized by casual acquaintances and perfect strangers alike. At some point, pictures of me will end up online, and Dad will kill me. There's a sort of satisfaction in knowing that it's inevitable. He just doesn't get my life. I need him to know I do what I want, when I want, why I want. I won't jump just because he tells me to.

I love him, but he can be a real asshole sometimes, particularly when it comes to getting his way. I wonder what things would be like if Mom hadn't died. If I'd gone to any college I wanted rather than busting my ass to get into Princeton since that was Dad's alma mater. Or, if I had earned something other than the MBA Dad wanted me to pursue. What would life have been like if everything wasn't always about what my dad wanted for me, but for once about what *I* wanted for myself?

Is it any wonder I pull these little rebellious stunts? I mean, I'm twenty-eight-years-old. I should be able to run my own fucking life. Right?

My friend, Tyler, looks in much worse shape than me, anyway. I'm only buzzed. I know how to pace myself. He, on the other hand, is trying to drink a woman away. Never a good idea. He's chatting up a blonde with a rack that could smother a guy if things got rough. Tyler's always been a tits guy. Not that I dislike boobs, but I don't go into a bar looking for the chick with the biggest set the way he does.

I'm not going to get in his way. Let him look for the most expensive set of tits he can find. Let him take a girl home and bang his ex out of his system. I'm just the wingman keeping an eye on him from a few feet away. Making sure he doesn't hurt himself or someone else. He can be an angry drunk sometimes, and the last thing I need is a brawl. Even I'm not that stupid.

I look around, squinting a little to see into the dark corners. The whole place is dark, really. Like beer goggles aren't bad enough, let's make sure the lighting is so dim a guy can't see his hand in front of his face. The bar is backlit in warm amber tones, and the rich, polished wood throughout the club just adds to the feeling of exclusivity. Only members can get in here, and they are carefully vetted. Not that weird shit goes down or anything like that, but the management likes to keep a certain standard. I appreciate that they have standards like my own.

I focus on a pair of familiar eyes and am startled to find them staring back at me. The so-blonde-you-know-it's-fake hair is the next giveaway. My stomach sours as it clicks that I just locked eyes with my ex-girlfriend. Judging by the way she hops off her chair and stalks toward me like a cat, she's been waiting for an excuse to come over. Just my luck.

"Hey, sexy." She folds her arms on the edge of the bar and bends forward a little, like she wants to give me a view down her skintight black dress.

Like I haven't seen it all before?

Like I want to see it again?

"What do you want?" I empty my glass and avoid eye contact. Instead, I look over at Tyler to see how well he's doing with his girl. She's hanging on his every word. Good for him. At least one of us will probably be getting lucky tonight.

"You don't have to be nasty."

I'm not giving her the satisfaction of responding to her tone of voice, but I can tell she's pouting. That's always her go-to when things aren't going her way. I might've fallen for it once, just like I had for that 'look at my cleavage' move, but I've moved long past it.

"I don't? That's funny coming from you."

"What's funny about it?" No surprise that she drops the childish shit when she sees it isn't working on me.

Well, the pouting anyway. Now she just sounds like a spoiled brat.

I toss back the last of my drink and wave over the

bartender. "You telling me not to be nasty, Trin. You're the queen of nasty, aren't you?" I trade my empty glass for a full one, not looking at her as I keep talking. "It's over. I thought I made that clear."

"You don't know what you want, baby." She makes the mistake of touching my arm, and I fling her hand off.

"Don't touch me. I wasn't kidding when I told you I never wanted to see you again," I snarl. What did I ever see in her? I used to think she was hot, sexy, funny, smart. Now, she just looks incredibly cheap. Ironic considering how much money she's spent on her looks.

Her dark eyes narrow dangerously. "Nobody talks to me like that, Anthony! Not even a fucking James!"

"Not even men you cheated on? I think that gives me the right to talk to you any goddamn way I please."

"One slip up!"

I laugh at her way of bending the truth. "A slip up that lasted four months and resulted in a series of sex tapes that would put some porn stars to shame." I shake my head. "Forget about it. Nobody cheats on me and gets away with it."

A movement around the corner of my eye catches my attention, and just as I notice a punk with a camera phone video taping our every word, I realize how loud we've become.

Great. I can't wait to see where the video ends up.

"Everybody thinks they're fuckin' paparazzi now," I sneer.

Tyler's fine. He's going to get laid and wake up with a hell of a hangover, both of which he can handle on his own. I need to get out of here fast before Trinity, or my secret videographer, or anybody else fucks my night up any further. I throw a hundred bucks at the bartender and rush out before Trinity can try to stop me. That will do nothing but turn into a whole new shit show.

Where can I go? I don't want that jerk following me with the phone. He probably knows who I am and thinks he can get some cash for the video, not that it's that big a deal since everyone already knows that Trinity cheated on me. I suppose it doesn't matter why we argued. Tabloid journalists can always spin a story out of nothing.

I turn up the collar of my coat against the cold wind and round the corner, eyes darting back and forth for a place to hide. Is this what my life has come to? For the first time, I wonder if maybe I should have listened to my father.

I eye a little shit hole joint where nobody in their right mind would ever come looking for me. Compared to what I just left, it might as well be in the ghetto. Perfect for waiting until I can get away unnoticed.

The place reeks of smoke, even though smoking in public establishments has been illegal in New York for years. It must cling to the ceiling tiles, deep inside the stuffing of the padded booths. I make a face. I have my vices, but smoking isn't one of them. I like my health too much.

There's jazz music coming from somewhere, and that just adds to the throwback vibe. Posters inside the entrance advertise live entertainment on the weekend.

This is a Monday, though, and the music is canned.

I perch on a stool at the far end of the bar, away from the door, and survey the crowd. That's a generous word, as it's more like a smattering of people. Mostly people in their mid to late thirties, but there are a few people in their twenties like me, including a cute little brunette at the other end. After my encounter with Trinity, I appreciate how natural and sweet the young woman looks. Not cheap or flashy, not trying to attract all the attention in the room. If anything, she looks completely out of her element here, which makes me wonder what her element is.

Normally, I'd go in for the kill, but somehow, that doesn't seem right. So, I watch her instead. I wonder who she is and how best to introduce myself.

CHAPTER FIVE

JANE

"I can't imagine how loud it must get in here when there's a live band playing." I take a sip of my vodka and cranberry juice and look around the bar area, where a handful of people are talking and enjoying their drinks.

"I like the vibe," Chloe says. "It's not full of a bunch of posers or hipsters or worse: aging frat boys."

I laugh, and it eases some of the tension in my stomach. I'm glad that she didn't drag me to a club full of people from work who would feel obligated to get to know me. After the day I had, Chloe's about all I can handle.

"That's good." My hands tighten around my glass as I search for something to say. "I like the music."

Her eyes light up. "You do? I *love* jazz. I can't play any instruments, but I've always wanted to learn. I can't quite force myself to do the work that comes with it, and what's the point of doing it if you're not great, right?"

"I like it better than a lot of current stuff," I admit with a smile, "but I don't know much about it."

"Oh, I can't wait to educate you. I know all the best places in the city. I dated a jazz musician once. Great hands." She signals the bartender for another drink as I blush, but I shake my head when she looks at me. I have to seriously kick ass in the morning to make up for my horrendous day today, and it doesn't take much to get me drunk.

"Do you mind if I admit something embarrassing?" She shakes her head, then takes a drink from her fresh glass. I feel silly, but I make myself say, "I'm just flattered that you would take an interest in me at all."

"Why? What's so bad about you?" She looks so honestly clueless that it makes it easier to answer her questions.

"I've never had a lot of friends."

"You?" She looks me up and down. "How come?"

I take a deep breath and prepare myself for whatever reaction I get. "I grew up in foster care."

There's sympathy on her face, but no pity. I sense she wants to know more. She's the sort of girl who always wants to know more, curious about everything and everybody. I give her what I can.

"My mom died giving birth to me, and there's no father named on the birth certificate. At least that's what my social worker always told me."

I can't bring myself to meet Chloe's eyes. It's better to get this out of the way now, I tell myself, before it becomes the sort of embarrassing conversation we have when the holidays are approaching, and I have to say that I don't have any family to go to. No family I want to see, anyway.

"I have a couple distant relatives, but none of them could take care of me, so I went into the system. I moved from home to home, always wearing hand-me-downs, and being labeled as one of 'those' kids by everyone." I run the tip of my pinky around the rim of my glass. "The county didn't have a lot of families looking to take in random kids, so we were usually stuck in the sort of places where there were always too many of us."

When I finally risk a glance, I see that she's smiling, and it isn't the sort of cruel smile I usually get when people hear my story.

"Well, we have one thing in common. We grew up in homes with a ton of kids. I have seven brothers and sisters, and I'm the youngest. Everybody's always up in everybody else's business." She rolls her eyes. "It can be a real pain, especially when you don't necessarily want everybody knowing everything. I mean, what girl wants all of her siblings knowing when she gets her first kiss? Especially when the boys all want to go beat the guy up, and the girls want to give you advice on your technique."

I can only smile in return. I can't help thinking that it would be nice to have a family who cared enough to be nosy. Nobody who grew up that way could really understand how lucky they are, because they've never known anything else. I'd give just about anything to have a family like that.

Her hand covers mine. "Are you okay?"

"Sorry." I force a smile. "My thoughts wandered."

She looks at my empty glass and shakes her head. "That's not doing it. You need something else."

I blink, confused. "Not doing what? What do I need?"

"Something else to get you out of this funk." She looks around. "I'm gonna get you laid tonight, girlfriend."

My heart nearly stops, and I squeeze my glass so hard that I worry it might break. "Um, no. That's okay."

She doesn't hear me. "I'll send one your way."

"Please, don't do this!"

But it's too late. She's already started trolling. There are hardly any guys even close to our age at the bar, and I hope that's going to be enough to dissuade her. I start sweating bullets at the thought of strangers coming up to me, trying to pick me up. I've never picked up a guy in a bar in my life. How will I even react to them? What do I say? I'm not like her, with a mom and sisters to offer advice.

It only takes a minute for the first prospect to approach. He's cute in an offbeat way, sort of dorky and shy. Is that who Chloe sees me with? I give him a shaky smile and feel pathetic for needing help scoring a man. I don't even *want* to score one, but that doesn't seem to matter. My discomfort clashes with his, and ultimately, it's a wash. After an awkward minute, I smile and tell him to have a good night, and he goes back to his friends, looking relieved enough that I know he didn't want to talk to me either. I catch Chloe's eye and try to look as forbidding as possible, but she's oblivious.

A few minutes later, guy number 2 comes over. He's a little more handsome...and a lot more aggressive. He sits close to me.

"What are you drinking?"

My nose wrinkles as his cheap cologne envelopes me. "Oh, I'm okay. Thanks." I take pains to sound polite in spite of my irritation. It isn't his fault that Chloe's on a mission. And I can't really be rude to someone for wearing too much cologne, can I?

"I insist. Let me buy you a drink."

He flashes a too-bright smile, and I feel myself withering a little under it. Damn that Chloe for putting me here.

"No, thank you. I'm all right." I slide off my stool and decide to tell Chloe, in no uncertain terms, that I don't *need* her to set me up. I don't *want* her to get me laid. I like her a lot, but I don't appreciate being embarrassed.

Only some guys can't take no for an answer. "What's your problem?" he asks as he follows me.

The bar is getting more crowded, and I elbow my way through the newcomers, hoping to reach my friend before Mr. Cologne Bath catches me. I tried being polite, but if he can't let it go, we're going to have a problem.

He's still going as he trails behind. "I asked what your problem is! A guy offers to buy you a drink, and you think you're too good for him? Who the hell ever told you you're so special?"

By this time, we're attracting attention and my face is burning. I should have just let him buy me a drink and leave it at that. Except guys like him, the ones who'll follow a girl across a bar because she doesn't want a drink, they think that once they buy a woman something, she owes them.

He steps in front of me, blocking my way.

"You're not that hot, you know," he snaps. "Ungrateful bitch."

I'm shocked into silence. I have literally no idea what to say to that attack.

As it turns out, I don't need to say anything. I hear a deep, resonant voice just over my shoulder. "There you are, honey."

I turn and can't believe my eyes. Anthony James is standing there, smiling down at me. That can't be real. Just like he can't be taking me into his arms like I belong to him, pulling me tight against his hard, unyielding chest. I don't even have time to gasp before he presses his mouth to mine and gives me the sexiest, most toe-curling kiss of my life.

CHAPTER SIX

ANTHONY

I don't usually do things like this. I'm not a knight in shining armor. I don't rescue damsels in distress. Hell, I don't even *like* damsels in distress. I've seen men treat women worse than that before. It doesn't matter how high the cover charge or how elite the clientele, jerks are jerks. And I never get involved because it isn't my business.

This time? This time feels different. Like I have to do something to help the brunette from across the bar who's so unlike Trinity. Maybe it's those wide eyes. Gray, I realize, not blue. They're so innocent. Sweet.

Besides, her lips taste like fucking candy. I've never been kissed quite like this before. An odd combination of enthusiasm and hesitation that makes me wonder about her. I remind myself to end the kiss before I forget my reason for kissing her. It would be so easy to take things too far, to get carried away.

Damn, I'd like to carry *her* away.

Her eyes are even wider than before, but I can see it's because she's stunned. I don't blame her. I just hope she doesn't slap me for trying to rescue her. That would be awkward.

"I've been looking forward to seeing you all day," I say just loud enough for the dickhead behind her to hear, and with just enough promise in my voice to leave no doubt as to who she is to me.

She's mine, buddy. Back off.

And to my own surprise, I actually like the feeling.

"Uh, yeah? Me, too?"

They come out as questions, which almost makes me laugh. At least she's smart enough to try to play along, even if she's scrambling to figure out the game. I find myself reluctant to move her away and then say goodbye.

"Come on. Let's dance."

The music has gotten louder, probably due to the growing crowd, and a few couples are settling in the center of a cleared area I assume is their version of a dance floor. I take her by the hand and don't wait for her to respond before leading her over there.

The new song is a slow one. *Perfect timing*, I think as I slide one arm around her waist and pull her close enough to leave no questions in anybody's mind. *Mine.* She's trembling a little, but her hands rest on my shoulders, and she doesn't step away.

"What is this?"

Her voice has a slight quaver to it, and I want to soothe her nerves.

I lean in on the pretense of needing to whisper in her ear just so I can take a deep breath of what she's wearing. She smells incredible, the sort of scent that fogs my brain and makes me forget I'm trying to be a nice guy. I want to bury my face in her hair and breathe her in. Even with the light as dim as it is, I can make out her pulse jumping in her throat. Something about that vulnerability makes her even more attractive.

"I felt bad for you out there, with that douche following you around, making a scene. I guess I jumped in before thinking it through. I meant no disrespect."

"Thank you for that. You saved me." She laughs shakily.

"No problem. There's only one catch."

She stiffens, a wary look coming into her eyes. "What's that?"

I don't like that, so I grin and hope that I can put her at ease. "You have to pretend you're my date until he goes away, otherwise he'll know we tricked him."

"Oh." She laughs again, a little more genuinely this time. "Okay. I think I can manage that."

She relaxes a little bit, but I can still feel the tension in her. She won't get too close. Understandable. I did sort of push myself on her, even if it was for a good cause. I need to make her see that I don't mean her any harm.

"You here alone tonight?" I thought I saw her chatting with a blonde, though I only caught the back of the blonde's head as she disappeared. Some friend, if she even was a friend. Why would anyone leave this girl alone here? Funny how soon the sharks start to circle when they sense a fish is all alone.

"No, I'm not. My friend is around here somewhere. She was trying to fix me up." Even though she tries to turn her face away, I can see the blush coloring her cheeks.

For some reason, that just makes me want to keep talking to her. To figure her out.

"Ohh, that's what this is all about. She was throwing men your way." Why not me, I wonder. I'm clearly the best catch here. Maybe the friend didn't see me sitting there alone. Maybe she saw me and assumed I was there with a girl.

Then I realize the more important question: why do I even care?

"Yeah. She was trying to, anyway." The girl frowns. "I wish she hadn't, and not just because that guy was a jerk, either."

"You don't like being set up like that?"

"Would you?" she deadpans.

I chuckle and turn her in a circle, making sure our bodies collide just a little harder than they need to when I pull her back. I wink at her when I do it and hope that it comes off as teasing rather than sleazy.

Then I answer her question, "I guess not, if it means some douchebag chasing me around the bar, calling me names just because I didn't fall for him right away."

"Eh, it didn't turn out *too* badly," she teases right back. "You're not a terrible dancer."

I'm not a bad kisser, either. I leave that comment unspoken, seeing as how she's still holding herself at bay.

Still, she has a playful smile and a gleam in her eyes, so she's not totally freaked out.

"What's your name, by the way?"

"Jane." She looks up at me like she expects a reaction.

All I can think is what a plain name for a gorgeous girl like her. Those thick chestnut waves and beautiful gray eyes. She has a delicate sort of face and a body with just enough curves to keep her from truly being petite.

After a moment of watching me, she continues, "I guess it's not very memorable."

She sounds almost sad, and I don't understand. Maybe she wishes that her name would be something more. Something elegant or exotic or whatever.

It's not a name like Trinity. Why am I thinking about her again? I don't want to think about my ex. Not when Jane is proving so interesting. She's not throwing herself at me, not giggling or flirting, and maybe that's why I want so much for her to open up. Because she isn't playing games. She's intelligent, beautiful, and she enticed me at first glance from across the bar. I want to know more.

She looks to her right, and I see recognition spark in her eyes. My first reaction is to assume that asshole is watching us, and I'm ready to turn and fight if it comes to that. Only it isn't him. I recognize the blonde who's staring at us with her jaw on the floor.

It hits me. Shit.

"Is that the girl you're here with?" I turn to Jane, who nods. "Are you kidding? Talk about a small world.

She works for me—at my company, I mean. Chloe. How do you know her?"

She blinks, unrecognizable emotions playing across her face. "Really?"

"Yeah, really."

She pulls herself away from me, just a little, and her face wears a tired smile. "You don't remember me? Guess I didn't make much of an impression after all. Maybe if I was still wearing my mocha."

Her mocha? My brain whirs a mile a minute...until I realize what she's saying, and it all comes together. Impossible. But now that I know, I can't deny it.

"You?" I ask in disbelief.

CHAPTER SEVEN
JANE

Well, this has been one of the most surreal nights of my life. I went from wanting to make a good impression on my boss to kissing and dancing with him—while he had no idea who I was.

I'm not sure how I feel about being so forgettable, but it makes sense. He's used to women far different from me. I'm just the poor girl he rescued from a creep. It goes to show how little our ill-fated encounter affected him.

He takes a step back, releasing me for the first time since we hit the dance floor. "Jane. I can't believe I didn't recognize you right away."

His words are smooth, but there's something on his face that tells me he's backpedaling.

"Well, we didn't technically meet this morning, did we? You were in a bit of a hurry." I know I shouldn't remind him of how rude he was, but I can't help myself.

He inadvertently leveled the playing field when he all but stuck his tongue down my throat, and I can't pass up the chance to have a little fun with him.

"I was rude."

"Maybe a little," I relent, "but you just made up for it, so I guess we're even."

He smiles at me, his eyes dancing. "Thanks."

And now it's uncomfortable. What do I do? He's not a normal guy. He's my boss. It's not like I can sit down and have a drink with him, not even if I now know he's a good dancer and an even better kisser. Just the briefest thought of that kiss makes my pulse pound dangerously hard, and I know I need to go before I embarrass myself even more.

"I think I should go now," I manage to mumble over the blood rushing through my ears. Between that and the music, I can barely hear myself think.

"What? You're going so soon?"

I nod. "I want to be fresh tomorrow morning. You know. For work."

He winces even though I don't mean anything negative by it. "Right. That." Suddenly, his eyes light up. I can almost see the wheels turning in his head. "At least let me see you home. Did you take a cab?"

I don't understand why he's being so nice right now, not when he wasn't this morning. Should he take the easy out now that he knows who I am?

I offer him another one. "Yes, but I was planning on walking. It's a pretty good distance." Somehow, the idea of sitting in the back of a cab with him is even more panic-inducing than anything else that's happened. If I tell him I'm walking, he'll back off. No one wants to walk that far in the dead of a New York winter, no matter how mild it's been.

Lesson One: Do not assume anything about Anthony James.

"I'm always up for a good walk. Can I walk with you?" When I hesitate, trying desperately to think of something else to put him off, he adds, "You shouldn't walk alone at night, especially in New York City. Didn't anybody ever tell you that?"

He has a point, especially considering where I live. I've just backed myself into a corner. If I tell him I'm taking a cab now, I'll look like a fool. And there's no way in hell I'm telling him that I didn't think of it being dangerous because I've never had anyone checking up on me like that.

I have a feeling Anthony isn't going to take no for an answer.

"Okay." I wave to Chloe to let her know I'm leaving, and the look on her face tells me I'm going to have a lot of explaining to do when we see each other in the morning.

Wonderful.

I wonder if I could try for a job in DC or Philadelphia. Or Seattle.

As soon as I step outside, I regret telling him I'd walk. I button my coat up to my throat and wind my scarf around my neck. He turns up the collar of his coat, which of course only makes him look more dashing. Like he needs any help.

We walk in silence for more than a block and it's

a surprisingly companionable silence, not uncomfortable at all.

And that's a lie.

He smiles at me like he'd rather do nothing else than walk in near-freezing temperatures next to a virtual stranger he'd been kissing less than an hour ago. The question of what he's going to want from me when we reach my building bounces around my skull like a ping pong ball. What should I do? I have no experience with this sort of thing.

Inevitably, I start babbling to break the silence. "I'm looking forward to learning more about the company.

He raises an eyebrow. "Hmm? Oh. Yeah?"

Maybe this is my chance to show him what a go-getter I am. Maybe this is a golden opportunity. I can erase that terrible first impression from this morning and get off to a better start.

"Sure," I reply, more eager than ever. "I mean, for instance, I overheard a bunch of people talking about Chambersmith this morning and how they're looking for a new advertising team. It's a pretty big deal, right?"

"Chambersmith? Yeah, I guess."

He guesses. They're only one of the biggest stationery and office supply producers in the country, and they're looking for his company to revive their image. How can he be so blasé about it? Then again, as the CEO's son, maybe he's the sort of person who's used to having everyone else do things and not having to think about how they get done.

Still, I keep going. "It must be hard for them, the digital age. Not as many people writing things out, nobody sending letters anymore."

"Yeah."

I'm losing him. Dammit. I have to make my point, and it has to be a good one.

I start scrambling, words pouring from my mouth. "I see commercials for them sometimes, and I think they're going about things the wrong way. Their approach is the same as always. Yes, we know their name, we know they have a strong reputation. They don't need to keep hitting us over the head with that. Instead, if it were up to me, I would make sure they acknowledged the digital age and how it's affected all of us, but also how some things never change. If anything, some people are starting to swing back to more traditional means. Like how traditional books are making a comeback after everyone said ebooks would kill them off. Bullet journaling is huge right now, for instance. There will always be people who prefer to write things out. There's something soothing about that. The same goes for getting a handwritten message in the mail. It's like, I don't know, reconnecting to something that's been lost. Besides, anybody who's ever gotten a card in the mail knows the feeling of gratitude that somebody took the time to handwrite a message. Finding that card or letter, years later, maybe even after the person who wrote it is gone?" I shiver, and not just from the cold. "I mean, that's huge. You can actually *touch* the paper, *feel* the impression from the pen against it. And you know that loved one, whoever they were, made that impression. Much more impactful than finding an email. Imagine finding a birthday card from a beloved grandparent and running your fingers over it. Imagine a commercial with somebody doing just that. I mean, jeez. I'd cry if I watched it. And I'd probably sit down and write a letter, frankly."

I'm pretty impressed with myself. In fact, I can see the entire commercial in my head. For someone who has no family, the idea of one tugs my heartstrings like nothing else.

If Anthony's impressed, he doesn't show it. He doesn't even respond. I wonder if he's listening to me at all. Well. At least it carried us through most of the walk. We're only another block shy of my building by the time I finish speaking, so at least I don't have to feel like an idiot for long. Hopefully, tomorrow he'll forget about this whole day.

"This is me."

We stop in front of my front door, and Anthony's handsome face is a blank mask. Shit. I should've kept my mouth shut. I should've walked and not said a word. He probably thinks I'm some scrambling upstart, trying to use our time together to my advantage...then again, isn't that exactly who I am and what I tried to do?

Can't I do any of this right?

He takes the slightest step closer to me. Shit. My heart drops. That's all he's interested in. He doesn't want to hear my ideas. He only wants to kiss me. Probably more. I feel like a rabbit in a snare, and my mind rushes around wildly for a way to get out of the situation. Meanwhile, his eyes meet mine. Wow. They're beautiful. He's beautiful.

I stick out my hand before those eyes of his undo me and I get myself into even more hot water. "Thanks so much for everything tonight. You saved my butt."

Oh, sweet Lord. What a stupid thing to say.

Something flashes in his eyes, and he looks down at the hand I've thrust in his direction. The corners of his mouth curve up into what looks like a wry smile. Then he laughs softly. Still, he takes my hand in his much larger one—his engulfs mine—and I remember the warmth of his hands on my back when we danced.

"You're welcome. I'm glad I could save, uh, your butt." He laughs again, but his laugh isn't unfriendly, and his eyes twinkle. Then he turns and hails a cab. Magically, one pulls right up in front of him. I've never been so lucky.

I don't realize until I'm already halfway up the stairs to my floor that he held the cab back until I was safe inside the building. I don't want to think about what that means. All I want to do is take a shower and curl up in bed.

And hope that tomorrow's going to be better.

CHAPTER EIGHT
ANTHONY

I can't forget her laugh.

I can tell myself all I want that she's my assistant and it's a bad idea to even *think* about her. I can tell myself she's so naïve, it freaked her out when all I did was take a step toward her when we stood in front of her building last night. Like she thought I was going to invite myself up or something.

I'm still unsure what my intentions were. I only know that she's the most innocent, interesting person and I liked being with her tonight. Aside from Tyler, I can't think of the last person I've genuinely enjoyed being with. It sure as hell wasn't Trinity. And even Tyler is getting on my nerves.

Dammit! I can't get that laugh out of my head, even with my father staring me down from the chair behind his desk. He's been pissed before, but this definitely takes the cake.

"Are you listening to anything I'm saying to you?" Dad's face is an interesting shade of purple. I'm torn between wanting to warn him against giving himself a stroke and wanting to avoid the sensation of getting thrown out his office window.

I decide to keep my warning to myself.

"Of course. I hang on your every word." Still, I can't help but be a sarcastic jerk. It's just who I am.

Purple deepens to indigo and I'm pretty sure Dad's about to explode. "If that's the truth, then why can't you keep yourself from making a fool out of me at every turn?"

"I don't think it's that serious, Uncle."

I turn my attention to my cousin Jerrod, who's standing off to Dad's side behind the wide desk. As always, he has a look about him that makes me think his underwear's too tight. He's shifty, squirmy, uncomfortable. And forever looking for a way to get a leg up. I doubt there's a square inch of space on Dad's ass that he hasn't kissed. If it wasn't for that...no, I'd still despise him. He's always been a snake.

He's also not usually one to defend me, either. I raise an eyebrow at this turn of events. "You don't?"

He shakes his head, and his slicked-back blond hair gleams in the overhead lights. "It was just a little squabble. A domestic issue. It could happen to anyone."

I narrow my eyes. Not helping.

Surprise, surprise.

"And get recorded and plastered all over the internet!" Dad slams the side of his fist against his desk.

I manage not to flinch, but it's a close bet. He doesn't usually let his temper get the better of him like this.

Then again, I'm the only person who gets to him, but only when we're alone. He's always in control around other people, even the rest of the family. Despite jumping at Dad's response, I get the feeling there's nowhere Jerrod would rather be.

"It's not that big a deal," I sigh.

"Maybe not this one thing," he snarls. "It's everything else leading up to this! This little so-called squabble is the straw that broke the camel's back, Anthony. I'm sick of the way you can't stop screwing around, no matter what I say. You were supposed to be *here* yesterday!" He pounds on the desk again for effect. "You weren't supposed to be *out*!" Another pound. "But you can't be bothered to do the smart thing, can you? You've gotta be your own man, make sure the whole world knows you do what you want!"

"Uncle," Jerrod mutters as he moves like he's going to go around to my dad.

"Stay out of it," I shoot back.

Dad laughs, but there's no humor in it. "At least he cares what happens around here! He does what I ask. I can count on him. Unlike my own son."

I manage not to roll my eyes too hard. It's not easy. Jerrod, meanwhile, looks like he's celebrating his birthday, Christmas, and New Year's all at once. His eyes are practically dancing, even if he manages to keep a straight face.

Ass kisser.

Dad walks around his desk so we're standing face-to-face. He's only an inch taller than me, and he likes to lord that over me whenever he gets the chance. Like it's some great accomplishment that he has any control over.

"I've had enough of your bullshit, Anthony. This is my only chance at getting elected, and you know it. I've been working toward this for years, and if I lose, there's no coming back from that."

"Yes. I know that." Who doesn't know it? The man's obsessed with the idea of starting a new political dynasty, like he's a Kennedy or something.

"But you can't help ruining it for me, even so. Isn't that it?" His breath smells like stale coffee and frustration. "If you don't get your act together, boy, I'm going to have to distance myself from you. You're limiting my choices."

That gets to me, even though I hate when he refers to me as a boy. No matter how many times the old man has threatened me, he's never threatened to disown me, and I know that's what he's saying, even though he's trying to soften it since Jerrod's soaking in every word.

"I'm giving you one. More. Chance." He jabs his index finger into my chest, and it takes all my self-control not to react. "If you don't hit a home run today, it's over."

"Home run? Today?" My mind races. Shit. What's he talking about?

Jerrod doesn't manage to conceal his snicker, but Dad ignores him. "Yes, today. Your pitch."

Oh, hell. The pitch to Chambersmith that I completely forgot about, in other words. I'm so fucked.

"Make it happen today, and prove to me that you're

serious about getting serious, or you're done. Cut out completely." He glares at me.

I manage to hold his gaze. I won't give Jerrod the satisfaction of seeing Dad talk me down.

"I will," I assure him with a smile, even as I panic inside.

CHAPTER NINE
JANE

I smooth a hand over my freshly-curled hair and check the time again. Where is he? It's well after nine a.m. and I tell myself that I'm simply concerned for my continued employment. After my 'talk' with Mr. James, I can't see him being tolerant of tardiness, especially since there's a big meeting today. What will happen if he gets fired? This will be the shortest and most pointless job I've ever had.

I wish I could get the memory of his kiss off my mind. Maybe then I could pretend that I hadn't spent thirty minutes standing in front of my closet, trying to find the perfect outfit to wear. The sort of thing that would not only tell everyone at James Enterprises that yesterday was a fluke, but that would make Anthony really *see* me.

Knock it off, I warn myself for probably the hundredth time this morning. I can't allow myself to fall too deep into the memory of that simple kiss. If I do,

I'll wonder what it would be like if the kiss kept going…and going…with a lot more touching. Like a whole lot more. Skin against skin. Palms sliding over the firm muscles I know are hiding under his impeccably tailored suits. His hands on me. Touching places...

And that's a bad idea.

Messing around with him, or even daydreaming too much about it, is a bad idea. Even if he thinks I'm a hopeless jerk for freaking out and freezing up, it's better than taking things too far. That kiss was enough. Now, it's time to get to work like nothing ever happened. That's what I'm here for. Work. To make a place for myself. To start building the life I've always wanted. This is my chance, and fantasizing about something that will never happen—that can never happen—will only get in the way.

My little pep talk to myself would be just what I need, if not for one tall blonde, very excited girl nearly running down the hall in my direction. Crap. I forgot about Chloe. I can't bring myself to rebuff her, not when she's been so kind to me. I want her to be a part of that life I'm building. I've never had a true friend, and I sense that she could be that for me.

So I take a steadying breath and brace myself for the onslaught of questions I'm sure are coming my way.

"What happened, what happened, what happened?" She sits on the edge of my desk and leans down until she's nearly bent in half. With her eyes sparkling and that eager expression on her face, she looks more like a child on Christmas morning than she does an adult. "Tell me! I've been dying since you two left last night!"

My cheeks burn with the heat of a thousand suns, and my bravado fails. "Nothing," I mutter.

"You lying liar!" She swats playfully at me, clearly misinterpreting my reluctance to speak for being coy.

I've never been coy a day in my life, but she doesn't know that. There's a lot she doesn't know about me, I remind myself.

"There isn't a woman alive who ended a night with Anthony James without anything happening."

Ouch. Like I need to hear that. I hurry to correct her assumptions. "Honestly. It's the truth. He walked me home. We shook hands at my front door."

Her face falls. I can tell she wanted more. It's like she was the one who didn't get any. I feel a pang as I wonder if she'll realize that our mutual appreciation for jazz is about all we have in common. Maybe it's better sooner rather than later. I learned young not to form attachments, and I have no reason to believe that adult life in the city will be any different, no matter how much I hoped it would be.

"Sorry," I whisper with a shrug.

She shakes her head. "And I promised to get you laid last night, too."

"Oh, please! Like I was going to hold you to that!" I wave a dismissive hand and hope she doesn't notice the panic that's bubbling up inside me. She's like a train running down the same stretch of track in a circle, over and over.

And I'm tied to the tracks, waiting to be blown into oblivion.

"Don't worry. I won't rest, young lady. Not until I've

found you the perfect one-night stand." She pats my shoulder as she gracefully stands. "I'm going to get you some action."

"Why is this so important to you?" I ask, a note of desperation in my question. I just hope she takes it the wrong way because the real reason isn't something I want to share. "Seriously, I don't need any action. I'm just fine as-is."

She folds her arms, popping one hip out to the side, a move that would look contrived from anyone else. "Nobody as gorgeous as you is fine as-is. You're young, and you shouldn't be alone in that tiny little apartment."

"I thought you said it was cute." I try to get her off topic because I would much rather be talking about my lack of space than my lack of a sex life.

"Life's too short," she continues like I didn't say a word. "You should get out there and have a good time while you're young."

As if she isn't only a couple years older than me.

Despite our similarities in age, I know that when it comes to sex, we're eons apart. I just can't bring myself to tell her why. After hearing about my sad little childhood and seeing my apartment, I don't want to give her another reason to see me as some naive country girl who's in over her head.

"I don't need any action, Chloe. Please." I pause, then add, "It's sort of personal, okay?"

Her expression changes to one of chagrin and concern. "I'm so sorry. I should've asked you if you're, you know, religious or involved or something."

I snort before I can stop myself. "I'm not religious. It's not a religion thing. It's a virgin thing."

Shit. There it is. It just slipped out before I could stop it. I remind myself that it's not a crime to be a virgin. I have no reason to be embarrassed. It's a legitimate choice and not one that means I'm weird. Just like no one should ever slut shame a person who has sex a lot, no one should look down on me for not having had it.

"You're a *virgin*?"

I would expect her to sound that way if she called me a zombie or cannibal. Like she's completely scandalized. Great. She's one of those women who think that a woman having the freedom to choose what to do with her body should only apply to the people who choose not to follow 'traditional norms'.

"So?" I look around to be sure nobody is listening, but I don't soften my voice. This isn't the sort of conversation I want to have at work, but I'm not going to let her make me feel bad about my decision. "What's wrong with that?"

She shakes her head, looking more shocked now than anything else. "I just don't get it. How is it possible that somebody like you could still have her v-card? I mean, you're gorgeous. Guys should be lining up around the block for you."

"I just haven't found the right guy yet, is all. I mean, when you've gone a long time, and you still haven't done it, it becomes a little more important to find the right person. It shouldn't be just anybody." I've rehearsed that speech so many times it rolls off my tongue like I really mean it. And it does the job, too, since Chloe nods like she understands.

Good thing. She doesn't need to know the real reason I've never let anyone get that close. She doesn't need to know about *him*. What he did to me. Nobody knows, and I want to keep it that way. Better to let people think I'm frigid or a snob or anything else other than a victim.

Just the thought of him makes me squeeze my legs closed as if I can somehow stop now what he did then. Sometimes I can still smell his cologne, that thick, choking reek. One of my teachers in high school had worn the same cologne, and I almost had panic attacks whenever he walked by my desk. Sometimes I can still hear his whispers in the dark, when I'm alone and trying to fall asleep. Turning on the light helps chase the memories away, but no light is bright enough to make me forget what it felt like to have his hands on me.

"Jane?"

I pull myself back to the present and remind myself that he stays in the past. He doesn't know where I am, and I intend to keep it that way. This is my new start, and I won't let him ruin it.

"I'm sorry I've been pushing so hard," she says, giving me a gentle smile. "Sometimes I wish I could go back to when I was a virgin, so it could be special. I completely get it."

"See? You know what I mean, then."

And thank God for that. I don't have the energy or desire to go deeper into the subject. She's far too easy to confide in, and I don't want her to see my secret every time she looks at me. So I focus on the part she can relate to and hope that will be enough.

"It's sort of a touchy subject," I admit. "And I'm not into the idea of just picking up a random guy. That's why I was so skittish last night. I didn't want to blurt it out in the middle of a bar."

Instead of leaving me alone or at least changing the subject, she nods, her expression determined. "And that's why it's now my mission in life to find you just the right guy. The sort of guy who will make it as special as you deserve."

Shit.

My mouth falls open. No. No, that is not at all what I want.

Shit!

As I scramble to try to figure out a way to stop her, she takes my silence as gratitude rather than shock.

"You don't have to thank me. It'll be my pleasure—and yours," she adds with a wink. "This is going to be fun."

I stare at her as she walks away. This is going to be *fun*?

For who? Because it sure as hell won't be for me.

CHAPTER TEN

ANTHONY

Well, it was nice having a trust fund. I might as well kiss that goodbye, not to mention everything else: the cars, the VIP treatment at bars and clubs, entry to any party in town, top shelf alcohol, and tailor-made clothes. It was a good life. It's all over. Hell, at this rate, I'll be lucky if Dad doesn't end my life, period. I'm fairly certain that it's only the law keeping murder from being an option.

What am I supposed to do? Besides wearing a hole in the floor of the men's room as I pace, nothing comes to mind. How the hell did I forget the presentation? Or maybe, just maybe, I didn't *forget*. I would have to commit the date to memory and prepare for it and actually give a damn in order to forget about it.

I am so fucked.

How could I be so fucking irresponsible? It's not like I have any real responsibilities. I sit in my cushy office and pretend that the things I do there actually matter when I damn well know that I can walk out the door and no one will know the difference. Except maybe to realize my father's stress level isn't as high.

Am I broken? Is that it? Why can't I get it together? Why can't I be the son Dad wants me to be—or at least pretend to be? I've spent so much of my life telling myself that my dad expects too much from me. I've let friends tell me that he's too hard, that I'm an adult and he needs to stop treating me like a child.

Except a responsible adult wouldn't be stuck in this shithole of a situation. A responsible adult would have put something like this on a calendar and set up reminders and actually done his damn job. I can make all the excuses in the world that lay the blame at my father's feet, but it won't change the fact that this is all on me.

I have an hour to come up with something. Only an hour to put together something that'll wow Chambersmith and his team of suits, or I'll be out of a job and an inheritance. I've never met them, but I can just imagine what they'll look like. Pretty much all the stuffed shirts start to look alike after a while.

What can I say that will impress him? What will get through? I don't even know their full product line, damn it. Why not? Because the playboy billionaire title I've adopted as a shield against my father has become a fucking reality. Somewhere along the line, I went from pretending to be a fuck-up to actually being one. What other explanation is there? I loosen my tie and ask myself if faking a stomach bug would be too much of a stretch.

I take a slow breath and close my eyes. I can do this.

I've faked my way through worse. Charm goes a long way, doesn't it? I tell myself it does and remind myself of the many times I've used charm to get me by. Surely I can make something up that sounds amazing but has virtually no substance. It shouldn't be too difficult for me. I knew all about looking and sounding good without having any real character.

Less than an hour later, I walk to the conference room, where Gary Chambersmith and his team of lackeys are waiting. And I still have nothing. Not a damn thing. Dad's not here, thank God. One thing went my way this morning. I hope it's not the only thing.

"Good morning. Thank you for taking the time to meet with me." I shake hands with all of them in turn. *Charm, charm, charm.* I make lots of eye contact, flash lots of teeth. They seem warm and willing enough. That's a good start.

"Is this it?" Gary's voice is a gravelly rumble full of disappointment, and his sharp eyes peer at me from over the top of wire-rimmed glasses. "I expected a team to come in and wow me."

Yeah. I could've put a team together if I remembered the presentation in the first place, but I'm as much of a loser as my father says.

I push those thoughts from my head and give Gary some amazing bullshit. "I thought you'd be tired of seeing the whole song and dance. You're unsure of us, so I don't want to waste your precious time with a lot of filler. It's best, in my experience, to cut to the heart of the matter."

That came tripping off my tongue pretty easily. If

the rest of the meeting went this way, I'd be golden.

"And what's the heart of the matter, young man?"

That's a damn good question. Time for some more bs.

"First of all, a strong social media presence. Our team is chock-full of young, savvy professionals with their fingers on the pulse of how today's consumer makes their purchasing decisions."

It sounds good to me. Not so much to them, if the blank looks on their faces are any indication. Not one of the six people sitting around the table looks impressed, or even interested. I see the last thing anybody making a presentation wants to see: the checking of watches. Already. We haven't even been in here ten minutes and they want to leave. I'm losing them. They're sliding through my fingers, and I have nothing to stop them.

Or do I? A flash of inspiration cuts through the fog of panic and I blurt out, "When's the last time any of you got a letter in the mail?"

The volume of my voice surprises even me, and heat begins to creep up my neck. Everyone else stops what they're doing to look at me like I just spoke Greek. I keep going before any of them can shake off their surprise and break the spell.

"Do you remember what it felt like to get a letter? Or even a card?" I focus on good old Gary, emphasis on the word "old." He's the one who'll remember handwritten correspondence best.

"I remember the way my grandmom would send birthday cards in the mail every year," I bluff. "I wish

I had appreciated them more at the time. It meant something, pulling the card from the envelope, seeing her old-fashioned handwriting inside. She had the most beautiful handwriting, too. Does anybody even practice handwriting anymore?"

That gets a few snorts, but the good kind. The kind that tells me I'm on the right track. That these are the sort of men who sit around bemoaning the state of today's youth, so anything that plays to that part of things will keep their attention.

"I wish I had saved those cards," I continued. "I wish I had something special to look at and hold. Something she picked out just for me and took the time to write a message in with that perfect handwriting of hers. You can't get that kind of feeling from an email, can you?"

"No, you can't." Gary's attention is firmly on me. I catch a few nodding heads in my peripheral vision, too.

It's working.

"The public already knows your name. They know you're the best, and rightly so since you've been working all these years to solidify that reputation. You have that logical side of things that tells them you have quality products. Now, what you need is a way to connect with the hearts of the public. You need to show them how important it is to hold onto those old traditions, and your products will make that possible." What did Jane describe? I search my memory, straining to get past the lustful thoughts I'd been thinking when I'd taken her home. I need to remember the story she told. "Imagine a commercial in which a little boy gets a letter from his grandfather. Then another one, and another as he's getting older. Then, we see that grandpa has passed. The adult version of that boy is going through boxes, maybe leaving for college or something, and comes across those letters. He reads them. He runs his fingers over the signature and smiles through tears. He takes the box with him. We fade out to your logo."

I'm sweating bullets as I finish. Huge caliber bullets. Can they see it? I sure hope not. I manage to keep my chin high and flash them a confident smile as they mull over the idea. Finally, after waiting for what feels like forever, I say, "That's just a basic concept, of course. We can flesh something out, maybe several somethings, to create a series of commercials based on the central theme of getting back to traditional basics."

The funniest thing happens. A slow, satisfied smile spreads over Gary's face. I'm almost afraid to hope it means what I think it means. Then, he says one word: "Genius."

I've never felt more relieved, not even that one time when Trinity had a pregnancy scare that turned out to be nothing. This is even better than that because this paints a hopeful picture of my future. The light round of applause from Gary's team just adds to it.

"We'll need a full write-up in two weeks, but I think it's safe to say you've got the account." Gary rounds the table and catches my hand in both of his and grips tight. The sort of firm handshake that businessmen use to gauge the measure of the other man.

The sort of handshake that I always sneer at and secretly covet. The kind that says I've done well.

"Excellent job, young man. Excellent."

Whew. I have to keep from hugging the old guy. Sure, I have to write up the presentation, but I have two entire weeks to get it done. It'll be a breeze...once I figure out how to create a write-up.

CHAPTER ELEVEN

JANE

"I don't need you to do this. I really don't."

Doesn't this girl know English? What can I say that'll get through to her? This isn't one of those situations where I say I don't want her help, but I secretly want her help. I'm not like that. I just don't know how to get her to see it. Not without telling her more, and that isn't an option.

"I won't hear of it," Chloe insists, putting her hand on my shoulder. She isn't looking at me, though. She seems like she's lost in whatever plan she's concocting.

"I wish you would at least try to hear it." I twist my fingers together, my stomach knotting. Much to my frustration, it doesn't seem to phase her.

She sighs, like I'm being purposefully dimwitted or something. "You're not some little girl living on the farm anymore. You're a city girl, living your dreams. Right?"

"Chloe, I didn't grow up on—"

She reaches over and grabs my hand. "It's time to get your feet wet, Jane." She winks. "Along with other body parts."

"Chloe!" I hiss. My face is flaming as I look around to see if anyone's listening. No one's even looking at us, but I still duck my head anyway. So far, my second day of work isn't going any better than the first.

At this rate, I'm going to die from humiliation before the week's out.

"Chloe, I'm serious. I'm not comfortable talking about this here—"

She waves her hand. "Come on, Jane. Everyone talks about it. You'll get over it. Just like you'll get over blowing your chance with Mr. Dreamy last night."

She has a point. I might be a virgin, but I'm not sheltered. Everyone does talk about sex like it's no big deal. I uncover my face. "You think so?"

"Yes! And those kinds of opportunities don't come around twice."

I open my mouth to ask her how she knows, but before I can get a word out, the man himself comes striding around the corner and heads straight for us.

Shit.

"Jane, I need you right now!" His voice is strident. No-nonsense.

Chloe glances at me. "Oh. Guess I was wrong."

I can already imagine how she'll grill me later. There isn't much time to think about that, though, with Anthony bearing down on me. There isn't much to think about anything, actually.

"Follow." He waves me into his office without another word or even looking in my direction.

I grab the first notepad and pen my fingers close around and dash after him into his office. He stops and turns his back to his desk, leaning against it with a sigh. I close the door behind me and try to tell myself that my heart isn't going a mile a minute.

"Is there something wrong?" I ask. I feel like I'm walking on eggshells. I want to ask him about yesterday. About the kiss and what it meant and how he walked me home but we shook hands and now I don't know what...

I feel sick.

He shakes his head, then runs his hand through his hair. "No. Everything's good. Too good, maybe."

I frown. "Is there such a thing as too good?"

He cracks a smile, but it doesn't reach his eyes. "You might be surprised."

Okay, now I'm curious. And grateful for the distraction. "What's going on? Can I help with something?"

His eyes meet mine for the first time. "Yes. I think you can."

Oh, boy. Does he have any idea what he does to me?

I should send him a bill for new panties.

Damn Chloe and where her mind has me going.

Just those eyes of his and the way his mouth quirks up in a knowing little smile as his gaze dips to my mouth. I want to know what he's thinking. If he's reliving that moment or regretting it. If he's wishing he would've asked me for more.

Shit. I think he's waiting for me to say something.

"Wha—what can I do?" *Get it together, girl.*

He rubs a hand over the back of his neck. "I landed my first account today." His grin is downright boyish, and it takes me a moment to realize that he's sheepish. Like he shouldn't be proud of what he accomplished.

"You did?" A burst of pride goes through me, and not just because he's my boss. Somehow, I know how much this means to him. He's more than just the boss' son, riding on his name and DNA.

He nods as he turns fully toward me. "And I have you to thank for it."

I point to myself. "Me?"

"It's Chambersmith."

Everything clicks into place. "Oh..." I don't know what else to say. He used my idea? He thought it was good?

He holds up a hand like he expects me to argue. "Before you get the wrong idea, believe me when I tell you I didn't mean for it to turn out that way. I never considered using your ideas—not because they weren't good, but because they were yours. Not mine. Only... well..." He trails off, and his eyes dart off to the side, away from mine, shame coloring his pride. "I didn't have anything they wanted to hear. And I needed this. I really, really did. You have no idea how much."

From anybody else, that would've been a line. From him, it's the truth. I remember the way his father looked and sounded when he talked about Anthony. I can only imagine what their relationship is like. Or rather, I don't want to.

He continued, "Anyway, like I said, I have you to thank. You saved my neck."

I smile and shrug. "It's the least I can do after you helped me out last night. I'm glad I could help."

"Do you want to do more?"

I freeze. "What do you mean?"

"I mean, I need help. I might have hooked them and even reeled them in, but this write-up they want in two weeks is what'll get them in the boat." His eyes are wide, almost pleading. "I don't know how to do one. I don't know how to present this. I need your help."

I'm thinking maybe I'm misunderstanding something here, so I ask, "I'm your assistant, right?"

He shakes his head, but then clarifies, "This is above your pay grade, I think—but not for long, if things go well."

That gets my attention, but I temper the spark of hope inside me. "What's that mean?"

He folds his arms and gets serious, showing me the businessman inside him. I have the feeling that if he would only get serious like that more often, he'd be unstoppable. That steely, determined look on top of his charm and charisma? Forget about it.

"Help me with this and I'll get you an actual job here. Not just a paid internship that'll end eventually, anyway. And not just a glorified secretary to make it look like I do something. You're smart, and your first idea was a home run when you weren't even trying."

I start shaking my head before he finishes his sentence. I'd come here with the hope of working my way into a real position, but what he's offering...

He takes a step toward me. "I think you're a sure bet, Jane."

I don't know what to say. He's putting a lot of faith in me, based on a single idea. Then again, what choice does he have? Who else can he rely on? His father? His cousin? Even in my short time here, I've heard about Jerrod, and none of it is flattering.

If I do this, it'll mean spending time together, maybe more time than we normally would. That's not going to get me to turn him down. The idea alone is enough to set my heart racing no matter how many times I tell myself to cool it.

Plus, a real job. One that will get me on the path to success a lot faster than what I'm on now. Who would say no?

"I'd love to."

A wide, relieved smile takes my breath away. Does he have any idea how gorgeous he is? Of course he does. But I can tell he's not trying to play me now. The man in front of me is the one I'd gotten a glimpse of last night.

"Excellent. Meet me tonight, and we'll talk about it?"

Why do I need to meet him somewhere tonight? Still, I agree. I'd agree to meet him anywhere, any time. "Sure."

"Nine o'clock? Same bar as last night?" And there's that impish gleam in his eye telling me that he's remembering what happened between us.

And not in a negative way.

Somebody set a bunch of butterflies loose in my stomach. "Okay," I whisper.

And pray that I won't live to regret it.

CHAPTER TWELVE
ANTHONY

For once, Dad's proud of me. Funny how I always told myself I didn't care whether he was or not, but now it feels sort of good. Especially because Jerrod is sitting to his right, and my cousin is most definitely not proud. In fact, he looks like he just sucked on a lemon slice. It's the cherry on top of my sundae, and it takes a lot of self-control for me not to brag.

Dad raises a glass in my direction, totally oblivious to the little drama playing out between Jerrod and me. I turn my attention to my father and mirror the smile he's giving me.

"To your first account and the stellar idea you pitched to earn it. I got a call this afternoon from Gary Chambersmith himself, singing your praises."

I return his toast and toss back the single malt scotch he ordered just for this occasion. Jerrod, on the other hand, hasn't touched his glass. I don't know for certain, but I don't think Dad brought him here when *he* scored his first account, and I know that has to chafe.

"So how'd you come up with the big idea, anyway?" His eyes narrow, and I'm sure he thinks he looks intimidating.

I shrug and finish off my drink. "It's sort of a long story," I explain with a grin. "Not the sort of thing I wanna go into while we're celebrating. Boring actually." Then, I turn to Dad. "So, did Gary confirm a meeting for two weeks from now?"

Dad nods as he finishes his own drink. "Oh, yes. We're all set. I'm looking forward to seeing what you present."

"Me, too," Jerrod sneers.

I take a moment to indulge in a fantasy where my fist is caving in his snide ferret face. Then I smile.

"I look forward to showing it to you." I check the time. There's still an hour until I'm supposed to meet with Jane. The thought of seeing her again outside the office is enough to pull at the corners of my mouth, making me smile just a little when I remember that laugh of hers.

I can't remember what Trinity sounds like when she laughs. Hell, I can't even remember if I've ever heard her real laugh. Jane isn't flashy or trendy or anything like that. She's real. Probably the most real person I've ever met.

And even the finest restaurant in New York can't make me want to be here more than with her. I'm planning on enjoying my meal, but I won't be lingering when I know Jane is waiting.

Dad orders a thick steak, baked potato, and side of

creamed spinach. How he manages to keep that trim physique of his is a mystery to me. Must be metabolism, because I doubt that when I'm his age, I'll be able to do the same. Jerrod, big surprise, orders the same thing. He's so pathetic it makes my head hurt. I order grilled salmon and asparagus, with a salad on the side.

And then remind myself to make sure to grab some mouthwash before I get to the bar.

Just in case I have the opportunity to repeat last night.

"You know, Anthony, I can't stop asking myself just how you managed to wow Gary Chambersmith, one of the toughest nuts in the world. You cracked him on the first try—not just the first try with his company, but the first try *ever*." Jerrod's smile is tight, practically splitting his face in two.

I wish it would. In fact, I wish *I* could split his fucking face. I don't give a damn that he's kissing my dad's ass, or even that he's more involved in the company than I am. I can handle all that. If he isn't so damn smug all the time.

I shrug. "Some people are just lucky."

"Luck has nothing to do with it," he snaps.

Dad clears his throat. "I beg to differ. A lot of our business is sheer luck. Hitting the right nerve on the right day at the right time. You catch a person on a bad day, and even the best pitch will go south, no question about it."

"I'm sure you're right," my cousin immediately backpedals. Dancing on a string, as always, with Dad controlling his every movement.

I want to tell him to grow some fucking balls, that I might respect him and his ideas more if they're actually his.

I'm the pinnacle of self-control tonight.

He continues, "I just have to wonder at Anthony's extremely lucky luck, that's all. Especially since there was nothing in his ledger only hours before the meeting."

I blink. Twice. What the fuck? I manage to keep from yelling as I ask, "You were in my office? Looking through my things?"

Dad frowns. "Is this true, Jerrod? Why were you going through his office?"

He turns roughly the shade of a tomato. "I went in to see if he needed any help with the pitch, but that was before we met with him in your office."

"Oh. I see." Dad digs into the steak that's just been placed in front of him, and I take the opportunity to glare at my cousin. At least the food's here, meaning our mouths will be too full for much conversation.

Or so I think.

"So what direction do you think the campaign will take now?" Jerrod asks before taking a big bite of his steak. It's medium-rare, just like Dad's, and he makes a face like he isn't enjoying it as much as he should.

"What do you mean?" I ask as I carefully cut my salmon.

Dad wipes his mouth. "That's a good question. So, Anthony, what shape do you have in mind for the full scope of the campaign?"

I'm at a loss, of course. What can I say when I have no clue what Jane's going to come up with? Vague. "I have a few ideas."

"Such as?" Jerrod lowers his knife and fork with an expectant smile.

Damn him. I check my watch and see that it's quarter to nine. "You know what? I have a meeting scheduled for nine o'clock, and I really should get going."

"A meeting?" Dad looks skeptical, to say the least.

"A business meeting. Just trust me. Hey, I didn't let you down today, did I?" I flash him a smile and shake his hand. "Thank you for dinner."

I don't give Jerrod the satisfaction of a glance as I stand and walk away from the table. I don't manage to get a good, deep breath until I step outside. That was close. I won't be able to sidestep perfectly reasonable questions for much longer. Jane had better have some great ideas for me.

The crowd at the bar is pretty much the same as it was last night, which means it's unimpressive. I spot Jane at a table by the wall right away. She looks just as cute as she did last night, and unlike most of the girls in the bar, she's not flashing any skin. Jeans and a fitted sweater that's surprisingly practical and attractive. Somehow it makes her even more interesting.

"Hey, there." I sit across from her. "You need a drink."

She grins. "You look like you need one, too."

"You have no idea." I signal the waitress, who gives me a provocative smile that I ignore. Jane orders a vodka and cranberry, same as last night. I order a bourbon on the rocks, then turn back to Jane with a smile. "Let's get down to business."

Her eyes widen like she's surprised. "Oh. Okay."

I raise an eyebrow and try not to crack a smile. It's nice to see that the chemistry I felt last night wasn't just me. She feels it, too. I'm sure of it. "Are you surprised that I want to talk business? I thought that's why we came here."

Her eyes drop to the table as color floods her cheeks. "Oh, no, of course. I mean. Yeah. Business. You need me for business."

I chew the inside of my mouth to keep a straight face. "That's right. I do need you. For business."

"Which is why we're here."

I'm not sure if she's trying to convince me or herself.

"Which is why we're here." I raise my glass in an amused toast to her and take a sip. She's far too much fun. And that's not something I've had a lot of in my life. Fun that isn't about getting drunk or hooking up with a one-night stand. It's enjoying someone's company, and this is the first time in a long time I feel like I can just relax with someone.

We talk for a few minutes about the scope of the campaign, if only so I can give my father an answer when he inevitably asks me. He will. He doesn't forget things. I love the way her mind works. She has that pretty, cute, sweet façade but underneath? Underneath, she's a shrewd firecracker. I wouldn't want to face her in a game of chess. Of course, I don't play chess, but I might be willing to start if it means I can watch that mind of hers at work.

"We've gotta hit them in the feels. If the big guy

went for it today, that's the direction we need to take. I promise he'll love it." We touch glasses, holding each other's gaze. There's something in her eyes I haven't seen yet. A depth, a wicked gleam. A part of her that I have an interest in drawing out now that I know it exists. One little vodka cranberry and she's loosening up pretty nicely. The night just might get interesting.

And it does, but not in the way I'm hoping. Because that's when the douchebag from last night comes over and grabs her by the arm.

CHAPTER THIRTEEN

JANE

"What the hell?" I can't help but cry out when a hand clamps over my arm like a vice. I try to yank myself away, but it's no use. He's got a good grip and has no intention of letting go that easy. My eyes go from his hand up to his face, and I immediately realize who I'm looking at, the realization sending a jolt of anger through me. Which is probably why my next question comes out as rude as I mean it to be. "Do you live at this bar?"

He gives me one of the sleaziest grins I've ever seen. "I knew if I hung out here long enough, I'd run into you again. Nobody does what you did to me last night." He squeezes just enough to make me wince. I open my mouth to tell him off, only I'm not fast enough.

Because Anthony is here.

"Get your hands off her, asshole!"

He lunges for the guy, grabbing him by the collar with both hands, and throwing him to the floor. The guy is so surprised, he lets go of my arm in time to avoid taking me down with him. I don't blame him. I'm in a bit of shock myself. Not from the idiot's behavior, but from the fact that Anthony has gotten physical with a complete stranger.

Over me.

"What the fuck is your problem?" The moron tries to get to his feet, but Anthony does the job for him, hauling the guy to his feet and slamming him into the bar. I wince as the bar rail catches the guy in the middle of his back, but it's more a reflex than sympathy.

"My *problem*, jackass, is when guys think they can touch women without permission." Anthony's right hand cocks back, balls into a fist, then slams home against the stranger's jaw with a solid crack I can hear even above the music.

And just like that, all eyes are on us, and no one is moving to stop them.

"Anthony! No!"

I want him to stop, *need* him to. He doesn't need something like this to get him into trouble, not when things are going so well for him. His father won't be happy if Anthony gets into trouble, and I definitely don't want to be the reason for it. As attracted as I am to Anthony, I need this job more than I need a crush on my boss.

He doesn't hear me. He's too busy splitting the guy's lip with a quick jab. He takes a third swing, a roundhouse, which the guy easily ducks. Anthony's momentum throws him off-balance just long enough for the stranger to turn, grab the first thing his hand closes over—which happens to be a bottle the bartender left sitting there as the fight took his attention—and swing it.

"No!" I scream, trying to warn Anthony in time for him to get out of the way, but it's too late. The bottle breaks over his head, sending shards of glass flying. He staggers, then falls against the bar.

Fuck!

Instead of taking advantage of the situation, the idiot runs out of the bar. I'm thankful for his flight or fight instinct telling him that the smartest thing to do is run because I wouldn't have been able to stop him if he'd gone after Anthony right then. But since he runs, I'm able to go immediately to Anthony's side, torn between wanting to yell at him for being so stupid and wanting to thank him for doing what no one else has ever done for me.

He defended me, so concern wins out.

"Are you all right?" I take his face in my hands and look at his head as his dazed expression peers up at me. His hair is soaked with bourbon—ironic since he was drinking it only a minute ago—and a trickle of blood starts running down his temple.

Shit.

"Where'd he go?" His speech is a little slurred.

Perfect. What if he has a head injury now? I know basic first aid, like how to make a butterfly bandage when you don't have insurance. Diagnosing skull fractures isn't in my wheelhouse.

"You might have a concussion," I fret. "I need to get you to the hospital."

"No! No way. Do you know the shit I'll get into?" he mumbles.

I scowl at him and put on my stern face. "Do you know what'll happen if you don't get checked out? You might need stitches, at the very least." I press a wad of napkins against his head, and they turn red as if by magic. I remind myself that head wounds always bleed more and it doesn't necessarily mean that it's bad. "Come on, Anthony. No arguments."

⁂

"It's a superficial injury," the doctor explains. "He doesn't even need stitches, but he'll need something for the pain."

"And there's no concussion?" I ask, eyes on the man lying on the gurney. There's blood on his shirt. All because of me.

Things between us just keep getting better and better.

"That, we can't be sure of yet. He'll need somebody with him who can watch for signs of a concussion." The doctor glances over at me from the chart he's reviewing and suddenly seems to realize that I'm not a family member. "Does he have somebody at home who can do that for him?"

"I don't know." I look at Anthony and hope I'm not crossing a line into territory that's too personal. "Do you?"

He shrugs. "Not really."

Oh, fabulous. The man might have a concussion because of me, and there's nobody home to watch over him. At least he's stopped slurring his words, and he can focus his eyes on me.

"What do I need to look for?" I ask the doctor before I give it any thought. I can't take Anthony to his father's, for sure. I wouldn't even know where to go, and besides, what will happen if he finds out why his son got in a fight? I'd lose my job and Anthony might, too. I can't do that to him. Not when all this is my fault.

After a glance at Anthony, who nods his consent, the doctor tells me, "Make sure he doesn't start throwing up. Try to talk to him as much as possible."

"Do I have to keep him awake? I always heard you have to keep concussion patients awake."

"It should be all right if he sleeps. Just make sure his breathing stays regular."

Right.

I sigh. It's going to be a very long night. A nurse hands over a bottle of painkillers, and before I know it Anthony and I are in a taxi and we're on the way to my apartment. My apartment! Of all places. I don't want him to see it. What'll he think of me? Then again, he's slumped against the door of the cab, in Happy Land. Between the head injury and Percocet, though, I don't think he's really going to notice much of anything. I'm sure that bourbon isn't mixing well with it. At least he only had time to drink one.

Still, I can't help the feeling of my heart in my throat as we walk down the hallway and I unlock my door. Anthony has never been here, and I'm almost nauseous thinking about how he sees things.

When a kid's in foster care and they're moving from

one home to another, most of the time, they're given a garbage bag to carry the few things that are actually theirs. It's not done to be mean or anything like that, but it's just the most practical thing. It doesn't do wonders for our self-esteem, I'll tell you that. Which is why I'm actually not thinking about Anthony's health for the moment. My nerves are too jittery for that.

If he notices the size, he doesn't mention it. He barely manages to stay on his feet long enough to hit the futon. I stand back, feeling helpless as my attention comes back to Anthony. What am I supposed to do with him? Sure, it's kind of funny seeing him so undone. He's always in control, looking good, charming my panties off. Figuratively, anyway. Now, he's practically drooling.

"Here. Let's get your shoes off." I sit on the edge of the futon and lift his feet, one at a time, pulling off the fancy leather loafers.

"You're so nice." His voice isn't very strong, but it's clear enough that I don't have to strain to understand him.

"Um…thanks? I try." I put his shoes on the floor. "Let's take your coat off next. The apartment might be small, but the heat works well."

I help him sit up and slide the coat over his shoulders. We're face-to-face, nearly touching. I try to ignore that fact even as it's all I can think of.

He doesn't ignore it, however. He leans closer and plants a slightly awkward and lingering kiss on my unsuspecting lips. My eyes fly open in shock, but I don't pull back. That's what I don't do. I tell myself it's because I'm so surprised, but deep down inside I know better. I'd been hoping for another kiss from the moment that first one ended.

When the kiss ends, he pulls back and looks deep into my eyes. "I really like you, Jane."

"You—you do?" I stutter. "For real?"

He nods, smiling broadly. I wonder for a moment if I'm seeing a glimpse of who Anthony must have been before all of this. Before his dad started treating him like he can't do anything right.

"You're special." He flicks a chunk of hair and then taps the end of my nose. "I'm not just saying that, either. You really are."

Wow, those drugs are really lowering his inhibitions.

"Oh. Thank you, I guess." My head's spinning. Me? I'm special? There's nothing special about me, not a single thing. And for somebody like him, somebody who's seen the world, to tell me he thinks that about me? No. He can't mean it. It's the drugs talking.

But he meant that kiss. That's one thing I know for sure. I could feel it.

I'm about to tell him that I like him, too, but I'm too late. He promptly sinks back onto the futon, stretched full out, and goes out like a light. As the tension goes out of his face, I'm struck by the innocence there. I lean toward him and brush some hair off his forehead.

"Terrific," I whisper. "Now what do I do?"

What I do is quietly change my clothes in the bathroom, then make a bed for myself on the little bit of floor space available to me. Only I don't sleep. How can I? He needs me.

I spend the night watching TV at low volume, checking on his breathing every twenty minutes or so—when he's not snoring, that is, which he does from time to time. It's a struggle to keep my eyes open the longer the night winds on, but I stay awake for his sake until the sun begins to rise. I figure enough time has passed by then to be somewhat confident that he's okay. I'm asleep before my head hits the pillow.

When I wake up two hours later, I'm alone. The only sign that I didn't dream it all is the lingering scent of his cologne in the air, mixed with the smell of bourbon.

CHAPTER FOURTEEN
JANE

There's a chance that I could feel worse than I already do this morning. A real chance. I could have swine flu or double pneumonia or something. Life could be worse than feeling so tired, I'm afraid to blink because there's a chance I could fall asleep in the middle of it.

If it weren't my third day on the job, I'd call out. Personal day, sick day, whatever. Any excuse. I've never gone almost an entire night without sleep, then been expected to put in a full day's work. An all-nighter before an exam? Yeah, but then I'd crash once I got back to my room. No such luck today.

For the second time in three days, I get on the elevator with more than one cup of coffee, only this time, they're both for me. If I could run a caffeine IV straight into an artery right now, I would. Still, I keep a smile on my face as I walk back to my desk. It occurs to me as I pass Chloe's desk—empty, thank goodness—that she'll just about die if she finds out I spent the night with Anthony James, even if he was unconscious for most of it. I can't deny, though, that I feel a little...*special* knowing I saw him at his worst last night.

And then there's knowing how he ended up that way. I can afford to smile a secret smile about it since he apparently didn't have any lasting damage. He must have a nasty headache, though. Hopefully, he has enough painkillers left to deal with that as well.

I can't forget what happened after that, of course. I haven't been able to get the kiss out of my mind since I woke up, and I'm pretty sure I spent my few hours of sleep replaying it again and again. The taste of him, the firmness of his mouth. It's the stuff of fantasies. Did he mean what he said about liking me?

There's only one way to find out.

The door to Anthony's office is closed, but I can see light filtering through the crack underneath. He's in then, despite the early hour. I gulp down half a latte before getting up the courage to knock on the door.

"Come in."

He sounds strong enough. I smooth my hands down the front of my dress before turning the handle, but it does little to calm my nerves.

I'd never know anything happened to him if I hadn't seen it with my own eyes. Gone is the slurring, stumbling guy who needed help getting his shoes and coat off. He's now sitting behind his desk and looks fresh, bright-eyed. The smile that lights up his face lights up my heart. It's like the sun coming out from behind the clouds. Suddenly, I don't feel so tired anymore. Knowing my sleepless night was worth it makes all the difference.

Before I can say anything, he speaks again. "Thank you for everything you did for me last night."

He's still smiling, which makes me scramble to put words together. That kiss is still bouncing around my head like a ping pong ball, and my heart is beating a mile a minute.

"No problem," I manage to choke out.

He looks chagrined as he rubs the back of his neck. "I hope I didn't act too poorly. I don't remember much after the hospital."

Everything in me deflates, and it's all I can do to keep smiling. He was on drugs, completely out of his mind. I should've known. I *had* known. Our first kiss had been a noble sort of thing, trying to save me. It's not any different than him hitting that jerk last night. Just the right thing to do.

Nothing more.

I can't let him see how it feels. Instead, I laugh it off—on the outside, even as I die a little on the inside. "Well, at least you don't remember my apartment."

It's better for him to not remember any of it. It's better all the way around. I try to tell myself this again and again. Maybe if I say it enough times, I'll believe it. Believe that it's better for him not to have to be embarrassed about kissing me again or saying what he said. I don't want things to become awkward between us simply because I can't let it go.

He only smiles. "How about tonight, we go to mine?"

I press my palms against my thighs and hope it

doesn't look like the nervous gesture it is. "To yours? You mean, your apartment?"

He nods, confident as always. Does it take being born into the world he was born in to have that sort of confidence? Thinking you have the world by the balls and nothing can stop you from getting what you want? It's an attractive quality. He has a lot of attractive qualities.

Shit.

"I'm obviously too dangerous to be outside with, and I'd like to give you a proper thank you—if you know what I mean."

And then he winks. He actually fucking winks. Like I need another reason for my heart to flutter and my knees to go weak. Can it really be happening? It seems too good to be true.

"You're sure you don't have a concussion?" I ask.

He throws his head back and laughs. "I'm clear as a bell. So? What'll it be?"

Oh, boy. I hope I don't regret this.

CHAPTER FIFTEEN

JANE

"I hope I don't regret this. I hope I don't regret this. I'd better not regret this. There's still time to turn back and pretend this never happened. He can't hold it against me. That would be sexual harassment, right? He can't risk that sort of lawsuit."

The words pour out of me in one long whisper that barely spares any breath. I shift my weight from one foot to the other as I stand in the elevator. I should go home. This isn't a good idea. I know it isn't a good idea. I'm smarter than this, aren't I? I may not have been born a city girl, but I know the way things like this work. I'm not the girl who wanders into her boss' apartment, all wide-eyed and naive, thinking all he wants is an innocent night of conversation.

The thing is I don't want innocent conversation. If I'm being honest, that's the real reason I'm still on my way up to the penthouse in one of the most exclusive buildings in the city, right across from Central Park. I want more. Much more. That only makes it worse.

So here I am, in the private elevator car that goes straight to the top floor. Where he's waiting for me.

"You can handle this, Jane. You're a smart person. You can be strong and not do something you'll regret." I nod firmly to myself as I step off the elevator. His door is just in front of me, and it's standing open. Am I supposed to walk in? Would that be rude?

I hate second-guessing myself.

"Hello?" I ask, knocking.

The door swings open further, revealing the most jaw-droppingly gorgeous apartment I've ever seen. Hell, it's more beautiful than all the houses I've seen in my life. The entire far wall is floor-to-ceiling windows, revealing a breathtaking view of the city. When I step inside, I see that all the exterior walls are windows, like a panoramic view. If I lived here, I would never do anything but stand there, staring out the windows. I'd lose my job. Then again, if I could afford a place like this, I probably wouldn't need to work.

"Hello?" I whisper this time, like it's a reverent sort of place, the sort of place where everything gleams and people must speak in hushed tones. My apartment is roughly the size of a corner of the living room, with its shiny wood floors and the glass-walled fireplace in the center. There's a fire flickering there, casting an amber glow on the tasteful leather furniture.

And I've only seen this single room. I can't even imagine what the rest of the place is like.

"Jane? In the kitchen."

Like I know where the kitchen is. I follow the sound

of Anthony's voice down a short hallway and end up in a spacious, bright room with shiny steel appliances. Surprise of surprises, Anthony is standing in front of the stove. I watch, slack-jawed, as he expertly tosses a pan full of vegetables in the air to stir them. Probably the sexiest thing I've ever seen.

"I didn't know you were going to be cooking."

He smiles over his shoulder. "What'd you'd think I meant by a proper thank you?"

It's a relief when he turns back to the stove so he can't see my cheeks turning crimson. Here I am with a dirty mind that immediately went in the wrong direction. The man only wanted to cook dinner for me. He hasn't lured me here to seduce me. I'm the one who's been seeing things that aren't there.

"I hope you like shrimp," he says. "I guess I should've asked first."

"Oh, that's great." My voice sounds hollow to my own ears.

He adds some to the pan with the vegetables.

"Have a seat at the island."

I see he's already poured me a glass of wine. White. It's crisp and almost fruity. I guess he took a clue from all the vodka cranberries I've been drinking lately.

Minutes later, he turns around with a platter of shrimp, sautéed vegetables and pasta in his hands. I applaud, and he gives me a little bow. "It's the least I can do after everything you've done for me. I'm afraid I'll always be in your debt at this rate."

"I'm sure you can think of lots of ways to pay me back." Where the hell did that come from? I wish I could reach out and grab my words and shove them back in my mouth. What's wrong with me, saying something like that?

He only grins. "I'm sure I've already thought of a few ways."

There go my cheeks again, burning like my face is on fire. I'm not any good at this sort of thing.

Time to change the subject. "What made you learn how to cook?" I ask.

He smirks. "Do you want the honest answer?"

"Um…I guess?"

"To impress women." He shrugs as I laugh. "Hey. No shame in my game."

I take a taste of the food. Wow. "Mm. Your game is strong."

"You're not the first woman to tell me that." He winks.

A pang of jealousy goes through me, and I tell myself that it doesn't matter. "I bet I'm not. I half-expected to find a revolving door when I reached your floor."

"The contractor's coming next week to give me an estimate for installing it." He shakes his head as he gives me a wry grin. "Smartass."

Are we actually flirting? I know I shouldn't, but it feels natural. There's a strange sort of easiness between us, totally unforced. It's completely new to me. Men like him normally leave me tongue-tied and wishing I were dead.

"Do you have any more dishes in your repertoire? Or is cooking a second meal never a concern for you?"

I sip my wine, which of course perfectly complements the food. Because he knows about things like that. Meanwhile, I usually go for whatever's cheapest since it's not like I have a lot of disposable income.

His chuckle sends a sexy shiver down my spine. "I'm pretty good with breakfast."

Fuck me. I bite my bottom lip and tell myself to stay cool. I want to hang in and flirt and have a good time. Dissolving into nervous giggles won't exactly do the trick. He's used to sophisticated women, not the sort of simple person I am. I toss my hair over one shoulder and then feel like an idiot for doing it.

"That's a shame. I don't normally eat breakfast."

Yes, because that makes more sense.

His eyes travel over my face, then further down to the little bit of cleavage I decided was safe to expose. "It's okay. That means more time doing other things."

The way he's looking at me is making it hard to breathe. I wish he would stop, almost as much as I wish he would never stop. Our eyes meet, and it feels like an electric spark crackles between us. I really hope he's feeling this too because I'd feel like an idiot if this is just me.

He's not looking at what he's doing as he reaches for his wine glass, and the liquid spills all over his shirt.

"Shit!"

It soaks in instantly, revealing the shape of his chest with the sort of detail that makes my stomach clench. I'm going to suffocate right here on this stool in the middle of his kitchen. It's official. This is how I'm going to die. Death by sexiness.

"I've gotta get out of this. Excuse me for a sec." He goes down the hall to a room at the end, unbuttoning as he goes. I tell myself I shouldn't look, even when he leaves the door open and practically begs me to watch as he slides the shirt over his shoulders and down his back.

Silly me, thinking it was hard to breathe before he was shirtless. There's no way he's real. His body is perfect, like a fucking fitness model or something. Like a guy from the cover of Men's Health. Abs that are the very definition of washboard, a back just begging for my nails to rake up and down…

What's wrong with me? It must be the wine. I don't usually think this way about any man, although he's not just any man. Maybe it's him. He does affect me in a funny way. Or it could be the way the city seems to surround me as I sit there in the lap of luxury.

Whatever it is, it's all going to my head and making me extremely brazen. Brazen enough to slide off the stool and march down his hallway. Brave enough to walk into the bedroom, go straight to him, and take his face in my hands before crushing my mouth against his.

CHAPTER SIXTEEN
ANTHONY

Damn. I didn't expect that to be so easy.

Not that I planned on making a mess of myself, but leaving the door open was definitely intentional. A stroke of genius—that is, if the fact that she's in my arms and we're falling onto the bed together is any indication.

I can't keep my hands off her. Her body feels amazing on mine, and she's so much more than the soft, mousey girl I thought she was. She writhes on me, the movement pushing her dress up her legs, and I nip at her bottom lip. She moans, her fingers curling in my hair as if she needs to hold me in place.

It's not until I run a hand up her smooth, soft thigh that I realize how much I've been wanting to touch her like this, ever since that night in the bar. I wanted to see if her ass felt as good as it looked, and it does, firm and ripe, dying for me to squeeze it and hear the way she moans into my mouth as our tongues thrash together.

Fuck.

Her long nails dig into my shoulders, and she moans again, a desperate noise that seems to go straight to my core and makes my dick surge to life. There's so much need in her, I almost don't know where to start. She's like a bomb just waiting to go off.

And I'll be damned if I let anyone else get to take advantage of that. Tonight, she's mine.

"Anthony!" she gasps when I break the kiss.

My mouth wants more of her. I need to see if she tastes as good as she feels. I trail kisses down her throat, feel the way her pulse throbs just under the skin. I lick that spot, then bite it hard enough to make her squeal. I like that sound, so I do it again, then suck the skin into my mouth until the blood rises to the surface. I mark her as mine even though I don't want to acknowledge what that might mean.

I move further down, hooking my fingers in the straps of her dress and pulling it down. She sucks in a breath when her lacy white bra is revealed and I glance up at her. She digs her nails in again. I'll be marked up to hell and back, but I've never cared less. I want her to mark me. I want to know how good I make her feel. Just like I want to be able to look at her neck tomorrow, even if she covers it, and know that she remembered when she saw it.

She wraps one of her long legs around my thigh and pulls me closer until my leg is between hers. I hike up her dress until it's around her waist and she undulates, back arching and hips pushing up against me. I press my thigh against her mound, my cock straining in my pants when I realize she's practically humping my leg. A steady stream of cries come from her mouth as I mouth her breast through her bra. Her nipples are hard, and I take one between my teeth, the fine lace allowing me enough purchase to tug on it until she swears.

I've never been with a woman so responsive.

I need more.

I roll onto my side and take her with me, giving me access to the zipper along her back. She gasps when she feels my hand against her bare back, and then does it again when I flick open her bra clasp. One-handed, thank you very much. Now I can see that her pretty pink nipples are even more delicious than I imagined, and I immediately latch onto one of them. I suck hard on the sensitive flesh, alternating pressure and teeth as I gauge what she likes best.

"Yes…please, Anthony…oh, God…!" Her head rolls back and forth, eyes closed, mouth open as she gasps and cries out again and again. Her body trembles, and I wonder if she's actually coming.

I can't wait to hear the noise she makes when I finally sink inside her.

I work her dress down over her hips, then down her legs, pushing up onto my knees so I can pull the garment off. There's an obvious wet spot on her panties, and my cock twitches. When I run a fingertip over the delicate silk, she bucks and throws her head back like it's the first time anyone's touched her like that. Fuck. I need to get to the center of her heat, the wet slickness I know is waiting for me.

I pull aside the crotch of her panties and mutter a curse under my breath. She's pink and glistening, with only the thinnest bit of hair. As much as I want to be inside her, I need to taste her first.

I cup her ass and pull her up to my mouth so that she's balanced on her shoulders and the top of her back. Her eyes lock with mine as I put my mouth on her. I lick with short, quick strokes, focusing on her clit until she begins to whimper, her hands pushing at my head. Only then do I give her a respite.

But not for long, because I'm sliding a finger inside her. She is so fucking tight and hot that I know it's going to be a fight for me to keep from coming the moment I'm inside her.

I use my finger and thumb together, working all those sensitive places. She's almost screaming now, riding my fingers as I stroke her clit and drive her closer and closer. I think she comes, but I can't be sure since she's raking her nails down my back and over my ass, bucking and writhing and breathless.

And so gorgeous.

I stop just long enough to pull off my pants, then settle back between her legs again in only my shorts. She groans when she feels my hard, hot length driving against her pussy as I run my tongue all over her skin.

"I need you," I groan, driving my hips against her. I just need to find a condom…

Suddenly, everything changes. Just like that. She goes stiff against me, and not because she's having another orgasm. It all stops like I flipped a switch or something.

"No." She pushes me away, palms against my chest. "No, I can't."

"What?" For a second, I'm sure she must be joking, but then she pushes again, harder this time, and I automatically sit up. I can be a bastard sometimes, but I've never and will never force a woman.

She scrambles to her feet, fixing her bra before pulling her dress on with shaking hands. Her face is white, except for two spots of color high on her cheeks.

"I'm so sorry." She won't look at me.

I just want her to look at me. I've never seen a woman behave like this before, and the fact that it's this particular woman bothers me more than I'd have thought possible.

"Jane, what the hell happened? Did I do something? Did I hurt you?" That's the last thing I want. I've never cared so much about whether a girl is happy or sad or hurt or whatever. Not that I'm a total *ass*, but I've never been the guy who cuddles and asks if it was good for her. This girl? She's done something to me.

I follow her down the hall, not caring that my dick is still standing straight out in front of me and I look completely ridiculous. "Just wait, okay? We can talk about this."

"There's nothing to talk about. I have to go." The next thing I know, she's out the door and on the elevator. I'm not one to beg or to follow a woman out of my apartment in just a pair of boxer briefs. Especially since that could possibly cause an arrest for public indecency. I have no choice but to let her go.

What the hell did I do wrong?

CHAPTER SEVENTEEN

JANE

Once again, I wish I could call off work. And I thought yesterday was bad. I only wish the worst I had to worry about today was fatigue. A night spent crying and reproaching myself didn't do me any favors in that department. So not only am I consuming more caffeine than is probably healthy, but I'm an emotional wreck, too. This is so far beyond that slight embarrassment that his rescuing kiss had been. This is total and utter mortification.

Like *why won't the earth open up and swallow me* sort of humiliation.

I'm sure he must hate me. If he doesn't, he must think I'm a hopeless prude who isn't worth his time. I can't explain why I froze up the way I did. I *know* why I did, but I sure as hell can't explain it to him. Not without exposing things I prefer to keep private. There's a good reason I keep people at arm's length.

It's times like this I wish I was never born, when I

remember that I'll never be normal. I never even had a chance. I don't like to think of myself as pessimistic or particularly maudlin, but I can't see any way out of this that isn't bad.

Maybe he's too angry to speak to me or even see me. And while I hate the idea of him being upset with me, I actually prefer it to the alternatives that mean I'll have to actually talk to him. That he'll want to avoid me as much as I want to avoid him is the only bit of hope that sustains me as I walk to my desk. I try to be as quiet as I can, not wanting to draw any extra attention to myself. I'm still the new girl, but I've had a lot of practice at fading into the background. I hoped this would be my new start, but it seems I can't ever truly outrun my past.

When I reach my desk, I can't really say I'm surprised to see that my typical luck is holding.

The pink Post-It note he took from my desk with MY OFFICE scrawled in capital letters sticks to my monitor telling me he's not going to simply pretend that nothing happened. Terrific. This is exactly what I need in my life.

I hold onto that little flicker of anger, letting it give me strength. I hope he only wants to talk business as I march into the room without knocking. Better to get it over with while holding my head high. I didn't do anything wrong, and I refuse to let him shame me for changing my mind.

"Good morning," I say when I enter.

He's standing with his back to me, facing out the window, and the only bit of his expression I can see is the reflection in the glass. His hands are clasped behind his back. He looks like he owns the world in his expensive suit and shiny shoes. Everything about him screams confidence, success. So why should he care about someone like me going cold on him at the last minute?

"Care to tell me what happened last night?" He doesn't turn toward me when he speaks.

I must have really struck a nerve. Male ego much? Sure, we were having a good time, but it wasn't as though I laughed at him, or fell asleep in the middle of things. And still, he doesn't have the right to treat me as if I did something wrong. People need to stop acting like stopping in the middle of something is somehow wrong. Wrong would be if he didn't stop when I asked him to, or if I went through with things and then blamed him for my choice. Or if I planned on filing a sexual harassment suit against him for how far we did go.

I didn't do anything wrong, I remind myself as I close the door behind me before speaking, though the last thing I want is to be stuck in his office. No, that's not the last thing. The last thing I want is for anybody outside the door to know what happened between us. That isn't the sort of reputation I want to have here.

"Like I said last night, I'm sorry if I gave you the wrong impression. What happened was a mistake. I shouldn't have started things in the first place." If I could just go back and undo that kiss…

He turns to me, and I wish I could understand the look on his face. I can't tell if he's wounded or angry or just plain annoyed. "You think I'm upset because you didn't have sex with me?"

I frown, puzzled. "Aren't you?"

He shakes his head. "I don't get you."

"What's not to get?" I offer, still unsure what he's thinking. "I'm a pretty simple person."

"You're about as simple as a Rubik's cube, and I could never solve one of those damned things." He rubs the back of his neck. "No, Jane, you're not simple at all. Because here I was, thinking there was something happening between us, and then you run off without an explanation."

My heart skips a beat. "You did?"

"Yeah. I was almost sure of it. I mean, I feel it inside."

He comes to me, and there's nowhere for me to go. I back away until I'm against the door with him only a few feet away. He doesn't crowd me to the point where I'm claustrophobic, but it's close.

"You have every right to stop if something makes you uncomfortable." His voice is quiet. "But I wish you'd tell me what's going on in that head of yours."

I want to tell him. That's the craziest thing of all. I wish I could unburden myself, lay it all out, tell him it's not his fault. That the person who's responsible for me being this way is in prison because another girl had more courage than I did. I want to tell him he's not crazy, that I feel it, too. Oh, boy, do I feel it.

Dammit. I was wrong, all the way around. I should've put up a wall between us and kept it there instead of being weak and falling for his charm. We could've been professional and gotten along well. I could've made a home here at James Enterprises, worked my way up in the company. I could've had a wonderful enough life with work and a friend like Chloe. I should've been satisfied with that future instead of trying to pursue something that I knew wasn't going to work. Not because of anything to do with Anthony.

It's all me.

"I'm sorry," I say again, and I watch the light go out of his eyes. My eyes are burning and my heart is in my throat, but I make myself say the words. Make myself let him go so he can find someone better. "I think it's better for us to work together and leave it there. Maybe, someday, we can be friends, but for now, we should keep it professional."

I fumble for the doorknob, turn it, and slip through the door before he can offer any further argument. He'll never understand how hard that was for me. He'll never know how much I wish I could've told him that yes, I feel what's happening between us. That I want to try to see if we can make things work between us.

He's smart enough to leave me alone for most of the day. Or maybe he's pissed enough. I don't know. I keep my head down and my eyes on five o'clock, just desperate to get out and be alone again. He's stirred up a lot for me, more than he could ever understand, even if I had the guts to explain it all. I want it to be all good memories and the normal fear that comes with starting something new. But I can't tell him that there are moments when I feel like I can hardly breathe, much less think straight. Too many ugly memories press on me from every side.

Which is why Chloe is the last person I want to see, even though it's been hours since my 'talk' with Anthony. I can't make happy or lighthearted for her sake today. The sound of her voice puts my teeth on edge, though it isn't her fault. I remind myself of that very fact when she appears at my desk. I'm pretty sure the smile I plaster on my face is more like a grimace. She doesn't seem to notice.

"I've been going through my contacts." She pulls out her phone and starts scrolling through. "I think I have a few strong candidates."

My head is spinning. She's good at catching me off guard, like she's always a few steps ahead of me. What is she talking about? "Candidates for what?"

She frowns. "For you, goof. Remember? I'm looking for the perfect man for you."

Oh.

I can't help myself. All the sadness and disappointment and pain come bubbling up to the surface. "Why can't you take a hint?" I snap.

Her frown deepens. She takes a step away, eyes wide. "Are you joking?"

Her voice is hesitant, and I hate myself for making her feel this way, but everything inside me is so raw that my walls go up automatically, even for her.

"Do I look like I'm joking?" I give up. This day is just too much. It's around three, and I've gotten all my work done. If there's anything else, I can manage it from home. I start packing up as fast as I can. "I told you I'm not interested, Chloe, and I meant it. Mind your own damn business."

Her jaw drops, and for a moment, I have the sort of vicious satisfaction that only comes when a person can pawn off their foul mood on someone else.

"Wow, Jane." She scowls at me. "You could have just told me no. You don't have to be a bitch about it."

She storms off, and I'm just too fed up to care whether I hurt her feelings. Besides, I did tell her no. Constantly. And she didn't listen. Is it my fault that she doesn't know when to let things go? She should just stay out of my business. Why can't the entire world just leave me alone? It never gave a shit about me before. Why is this any different?

I do my own storming off, not even bothering to tell Anthony I'm leaving, much less ask whether it's okay to go. I wonder if he'll even notice I'm gone. If anyone will for that matter.

CHAPTER EIGHTEEN
ANTHONY

"Man, I need to get out tonight."

I'm glad Tyler's only on the phone so he can't see when I roll my eyes. He's going to have to get over his girl eventually or stop using her as an excuse to go out every night. My patience with him is finally wearing thin.

"Did you hear anything I just said?" I ask, my voice edged with annoyance.

I've spent the past twenty minutes telling him about Jane, and all he can think about is wanting to go out because his girlfriend dumped him a month ago. I feel bad for him, but it took a lot for me to share with him like that. I mean, we're close, and I would do anything for him, but that doesn't mean I enjoy baring my soul. That would be why I don't do it much, and he knows it. I don't ask for much in my friendships, but this one time, I wish he would actually think about someone other than himself.

He sighs, and I can almost hear him rolling his eyes. "Maybe you should let me finish."

I frown but say, "Okay. Go ahead."

"I was gonna say, I need to get out tonight and so do you. You need to get laid, buddy. Get that girl out of your head." He says it like it's going to be easy.

Except I'm not sure getting laid will do it. It's Monday, four days after the last time I saw her in my office, and I sure as hell haven't stopped thinking about her. I can't get the taste of her skin off my mind, the sound of her voice as she moaned my name. There's an email sitting up on my monitor, and it's from her. It's completely professional and totally lacking, as if what happened between us was erased from her memory. She's not kidding. She really wants to forget all of it, to the point where she's willing to risk her job by calling off for two days.

The worst part is, she's brilliant. I can't even get mad at her for not being around because she's still doing all the work she needs to do, and she's sharing ideas with me. They're all genius, which I know means she's an amazing asset for the company. But that's all she'll give me. No answers, no explanations. Every time I ask a question that isn't business related, she ignores it. She won't even tell me why she won't come to work, even though I know very well why. She isn't as unaffected as she pretends. She can't see me and still keep her distance. I could make a big deal about it, but I know damn well if I go to HR about Jane's attendance, she could counter with my behavior making for a hostile work environment, and that's the sort of press my father might very well use as an excuse to kill me.

As always, Tyler has some pretty strong opinions. Which I'm sure aren't colored at all by his own recent romantic issues. "Dude. She's crazy. I mean, she practically threw herself at you and then she acted all nuts and ran off. She doesn't know what she wants. Forget about her and come out with me tonight. Get some ass. You won't even remember her in the morning."

I doubt it, but I agree anyway. It's not like I've never regretted agreeing to something Tyler wants to do. At least I won't be sitting at home on my couch, replaying that night over and over, trying to figure out when things went wrong. Or, worse, fantasizing about how things would have progressed if I'd done one thing or another differently.

I need to avoid going home as much as possible. If nothing else, being with Tyler gives me an excuse to get drunk on a work night. At least an excuse that's better than me drinking alone in the dark in my apartment.

Why not. Things can't possibly get any worse.

Hours later, he sidles up to me with a frown. "What's your problem, man? You need another drink?"

I shake my head and wish I had gone home after work instead of going out to the club. Drinking in the dark holds more appeal right now than all of this. Not that I can explain it to him. Hell, I can't explain it to myself.

"Nah. I don't know. I'm just not into it tonight." I try to shrug it off. Would it be ridiculous if I tell him I have a headache?

Tyler glances at the girl I just turned away as she walks back to the table full of her friends. She's hot—smokin' hot. Tall, leggy, with pouty lips I would normally imagine sliding up and down my dick within about three seconds of talking with her. When she came over and introduced herself, I didn't feel anything. I haven't felt anything all night, actually. Not for any of the girls who've given me the eye or "accidentally" bumped into me. I've been turning down ass all night. And he knows how unlike me that is. *I* know how unlike me that is.

"You've got it bad, brother." He has a smug sort of smirk on his face as he raises a glass in a toast. The douche is lucky we're out in public, where I can't get away with hitting him.

I'm lucky nothing came out about the fist fight I got in over Jane, and a second brawl would be pushing my luck. Dad's finally not treating me like a disappointment, and getting a shot in at Tyler isn't worth losing that.

"I don't have anything bad. I'm just not in the mood tonight. Is it against the law for me not to be in the mood to fuck around?" I finish my drink in a single gulp and decide that the buzz I have isn't enough.

"Then you're getting old, Anthony. It's one or the other."

"Fine. I'm getting old." I turn away from him and look over the room again because it's easier to do that than to keep listening to my best friend trying to get under my skin. Did I give him shit when he broke up and the whole world ended? No. I was there as his friend. I'm glad he thinks it's so funny that I'm going through something I've never dealt with before.

Someone catches my attention from across the room. A curvy blonde is taking off her jacket by the door, and I can't help dipping my gaze down to check out her ass.

Killer.

If she looks that good from behind, I can make it work. She wouldn't be the first woman I preferred to take doggy-style because that showed off her best assets. Some women might think that makes me a pig, but I'm always upfront that all I'm looking for is sex. That's what tonight's about too, right? The sort of fucking that will push aside any lingering attraction I have for Jane.

Which means a blonde is best since I don't think I can be with a brunette right now and not think of Jane. Of how I want to have her on her knees in front of me, my hand tangled in her hair as she takes me in her mouth. Her hair spread out on my pillow as I move above her. Those wide gray eyes glazed with pleasure... fuck.

Tyler's right. I need to get laid.

I turn my attention back to the blonde just as she turns around. I'm already psyching myself up to go over to her when I realize that I know those eyes, and that smile, and every inch of her paid-for curves.

Trinity. And she's coming my way.

I should turn away from her, make it clear that I'm not checking her out. I should make sure Tyler keeps his mouth shut about why we're here, because as much as he dislikes Trinity, with as many shots as he's been knocking back, he might think it's a good idea to mention my recent women troubles.

Trinity will bring me nothing but grief. I know this as much as I know that pretty much anyone I hook up with tonight is going to pale in comparison to Jane. Which means no one is going to be exactly what I'm looking for, and it'll only be for tonight. We'll go to a hotel, fuck, and then I'll leave as soon as we're done. I'll tell whoever I'm with that she can stay the night, then take off before she can ask any questions. That won't work with Trinity since she knows where I live. And she might come into things expecting us to go back to the way we were.

But isn't there something to be said for the devil we know? At least I know what I'm getting myself into with that one. I can make sure I'm clear about this only being a random hook-up, a one-time thing, and if she doesn't accept that, I'll walk away. And if she says she accepts it, then changes her mind, that's on her, not me. Whatever little scenario her mind may cook up is her responsibility, not mine.

So why is this a bad idea?

Hell, it might even be kismet, her being here tonight. And who am I to say no to fate?

CHAPTER NINETEEN
JANE

I should get used to being alone. I'll be alone for the rest of my life, after all. I mean, if I can't manage to put my past aside for a guy I really like, a guy as amazing as Anthony, then I'll never be able to be with anyone. I should've known better. I mean, the first guy who ever tried to kiss me, I slapped. And then when, even after that, Clay Shore got up enough nerve to ask me out, I freaked. Once that story made the rounds, no one bothered me again.

At least the sound of the TV keeps me company now. I'm lucky I found one so cheap, otherwise, silence might be my only companion. I lean against the window frame and peer through the cloudy old glass to the street below. It's raining, nasty-looking. The sort of winter day that makes even me hate the winter. I usually like snow and cold, bundling up inside with some hot cocoa.

I can feel the cold seeping through the gaps between

the glass and the wood, and I shiver. I wrap my arms around myself, the thick cardigan I pulled on over my pajamas at least keeping me moderately comfortable, though definitely not fashionable. What does it matter? Nobody will see me. Nobody's seen me in days, though that's going to have to change soon. I'll eventually run out of groceries and have to venture outside. That's when I'll worry about looking presentable.

The city is moving from late afternoon to early evening as I watch. All the street lamps are on already, and talk shows have changed to local news. The news is my main connection to the outside world after cutting myself off for days. I'm going to have to get back into the world soon. I don't have a choice. I wish I did. I wish I could just order everything online and never have to leave my apartment.

Healthy, I know. I took a few psychology classes in college, telling myself that they would be good to help me figure out marketing stuff. Knowing how people think, why they think the way they do. And it made sense at the time, but even as I sat in one class after another, I knew the real reason I signed up for all those classes outside my major.

I wanted to figure myself out. Wanted to find a way to heal what's broken. I still do want that, but I've since accepted that it will never happen. I can't fix what's wrong with me, and I can't trust anyone else to do it either.

A knock at the door shakes me out of my stupor. Crap. I'll just ignore it. I go back to looking out the window, intent on forgetting I ever heard anything. Nobody visits me, anyway. They probably got the wrong door, and they'll realize it when I don't answer or when they text whoever they're supposed to be meeting...

"Jane? I know you're home. I hear the TV on in there."

Shit.

I can't decide if I'm annoyed with Chloe or glad that she's tenacious. I've been sick with guilt over the way I talked to her. She doesn't know any other way to be, and I already knew that. She's this way with everyone. Nobody ever told her there are situations that can't be smoothed over with a forceful personality or charm.

I must hesitate too long, because she continues. "Come on. Please. Let me in. I came to make peace."

It's not her fault, I remind myself, as I open the door. It's not anybody's fault but his. My uncle's face is in my head as I open the door to find Chloe holding up a six pack of beer. "I come with gifts. I'm sorry. It hasn't been the same at the office without you."

I can't help but smile in spite of myself. She's so genuine that I feel even worse about how I behaved. "I've only worked there for a week. How can you say that?"

She shrugs. "It's true, though. I miss you around the place."

How can I turn her away? Instead, I step aside to let her in, then sit next to her and take the beer she offers me. I don't usually drink beer—just the scent is enough to send my mind places I don't want it to go—but I need a drink if I'm going to get through my story.

Maybe I've found someone to trust after all. Or maybe I've just reached a place in my life that what I need is so big that I'm desperate for someone to talk to. Chloe could be my friend, if I let myself trust her.

"I'm sorry I acted so crazy back at the office," I say as I look down into the bottle's neck. I can't look at her just now. "I've been feeling bad about it ever since. You didn't deserve it. You don't know what's really going on with me because I didn't tell you, so I can't hold you to anything."

She's uncharacteristically subdued when she replies, "You don't need to tell me. I'll mind my business. You were right. I should've listened to you when you said you didn't want me setting you up."

But I shake my head. I need to tell her—if not her, then who? I don't have anyone else. "I'm so tired of keeping it all to myself. It's heavy, and I can't carry it all on my own anymore." My voice is surprisingly steady.

She puts her hand on my arm and gives it a compassionate squeeze. "Then I'm here." Her expression is earnest. "I know I sound like I never take anything serious, but I'm here for you, Jane. Whatever you need. And I promise I'll listen this time."

I believe her. And maybe that's why I tell my story for the first time ever.

I start slow, which surprises me. I always thought when I let someone in on this part of my life it'd come out in a rush, but that's not the case.

"I told you about my parents' and how I grew up in a foster home, but I didn't tell you that I did have an uncle. Kind of. He used to come through town every once in a while. He was my mom's half-brother, or at least that's what he said. His job meant he was always traveling, which was the reason he gave for not being able to take care of me when she died. I don't know how much of what he said was true, but he must've been able to prove it because he had it all arranged with my social worker that whenever he was in town, he could spend time with me. It was only once or twice a year from about seven until I was thirteen, and it always felt awkward." I take a deep, shaky breath. I could stop now, make up some lie or excuse, but Chloe is there, and she's listening, so I continue, "On my birthday that year, he came by. We went to a bar, which seemed beyond strange to me. I was only a kid, you know? But he was my only connection to my 'real' family. He got drunk, and it got really late and the other guys in the bar were looking at me..."

"Oh, my God," Chloe whispers. Her hand tightens on mine like she knows what's coming.

I close my eyes, but they pop back open almost immediately when *he's* there. "When we got into his car, he grabbed me. Tried to kiss me. I turned my head, but he slobbered all over my face and started groping me. First over my sweatshirt, then he started trying to get under it, then between my legs..."

"Jane..."

"He didn't...I mean it didn't get *that* far. But it wasn't for lack of trying. Thank God I was wearing jeans. He could barely get his fly down, and then he couldn't get... *it* up. He tried, and then he grabbed my hand and put it..." I swallowed hard and felt Chloe's fingers dig into my arm. "I fought him off and got out of the car and ran all the way back to the house. It was a few miles, but I barely noticed. I was just so glad to be away from him. He never came back, and I never asked about him." I squeeze my eyes shut and shake my head. My hands are in fists, but I actually feel a bit lighter. "I've never felt comfortable with men since then. I hate being alone with them. I seize right up...if I'm not freaking the fuck out. And that's why…you know. Why I'm still a virgin."

The next thing I know her arms are around me, and it's the first real hug I ever remember getting. "I'm so sorry, Jane. I didn't mean to push you the way I did. I never would have if I'd known..."

All the fight I had goes out of me. I lean against her and allow myself to accept the comfort she's trying to offer. "Thank you, Chloe. I've never told anyone...never had anyone *to* tell."

"I'm glad you told me." Her embrace tightens. "Thank you for trusting me."

She finally sits back, taking my hands between hers. I wonder if this is what having a sister could be like.

I'm the one who breaks the silence. There's one more secret I need to share. "The worst part is, you know how you kept talking about helping me find the right guy? I think I finally did. But I can't let myself be open with him."

"You did?" She sits up, and there's interest in her eyes though she manages to reign herself in. She's learning. The less I'm pushed, the more I share willingly.

"Well..." I look at her from the corner of my eye to gauge her reaction. "It's Anthony."

Her jaw drops, and for several full seconds, she's

actually speechless. Which, I'm sure, is the first time. "*What*? As in Anthony *James*?"

I nod, then tell her everything that happened, right down to the last moments in his bed. Well, almost everything. I refrain from anything graphic—and I might leave out some of the more embarrassing noises I made—but she doesn't seem to mind. She's too busy staring at me with wide eyes, drinking in every detail. By the time I'm done, she holds her head in her hands.

"I—I can't believe it."

"You don't have to sound so surprised." I smile. I like having a friend.

"You know I don't mean it that way." She rolls her eyes, a friendly grin curving her lips. "Wow. You and Anthony."

"Me and nobody," I remind her.

"You don't know that."

"I do know it. I blew it. You weren't there. How patient is a man like him supposed to be? And the more time that's passed, the worse it is. I just can't bring myself to face him again. I'm so embarrassed, and I don't know how to tell him."

"Listen. I'll go with you to find him, if it'll make you feel better. I think you should try to tell him. If only to make it right for you." She squeezes my hands. "You can trust him."

I nod slowly even though I'm not entirely sure that she's right. Not about trusting him, because that's something I know for certain. He's already proven that by confessing that he used my ideas for Chambersmith. And not about whether or not I should tell him, but if I'm strong enough to do it.

CHAPTER TWENTY

ANTHONY

I can't believe this is happening. But no matter how many times I tell myself to stop, I can't. I won't. I need to forget about how much I wish it's another woman in my arms. With Trinity writhing around in my lap, rubbing herself against the growing bulge just below my belt, it's as good a way as any.

And less of a hangover than drinking myself to oblivion would be.

"Mmm...baby..."

She sighs as I run my mouth over the skin of her throat. She smells good. Familiar. There's something to be said for familiarity. She's just what I need to forget about Jane. The thought of *her* makes me hold onto Trinity even tighter. The blonde groans and grinds against my dick, running her hands through my hair, pulling my mouth away from her throat so she can thrust her tongue between my lips. It's nothing new, but my body responds. Hell, maybe my body responds *because* it's the same old thing that I'm used to.

It's not just what she's doing to me. I know just how to touch her to drive her nuts, the way to run my hands up her thighs and over her ass to get her to moan. I dig my fingers into her soft flesh and groan. She's so ready for me. There's no question about that. The back corner of the club is just dark enough for us to get away with what we're doing without being noticed, but I don't think I could get away with much more without risking getting thrown out. A shame, because I'd love to just pull aside those panties and slide into her, lose myself and all memories of anything—or anyone—else.

Dammit!

Again, I'm thinking about *her*. I can't stop. I have another woman in my lap, a beautiful woman whose hand is sliding between us to massage my dick as our tongues twist together, but I can't stop thinking about fucking Jane Ward. It's not her hand or her tongue or her body. It's not her.

And I feel myself going a little soft.

Shit.

"What's wrong?" she whispers in my ear before biting on the lobe.

What *is* wrong? That's a good question. I wish I could give Trinity some great excuse about this place being too public, but I know she'd see through that shit. In the past, all that would mean was we needed to find somewhere a bit more private. I wouldn't be losing an erection because of it.

And part of me doesn't even want to look for a reason, because that could mean having to look a little too closely at some things I don't want to look at.

Even trying to not think about it, I'm suddenly not as interested in any of this as I was just a few seconds ago. She hasn't quite figured it all out yet, though. She's writhing around even harder, stroking me, sighing and moaning, trying to revive my interest. And it's not working.

If anything, it's just getting worse.

I pull back with a frustrated sigh. "We have to stop."

"What?" Her voice is thick and breathy with desire, but all it does is annoy me.

"I said we have to stop." I push her hand away and then grab her hips, physically moving her off my lap. She lands next to me in the booth, mouth open, eyes wide.

Her lipstick is smudged, and I scrub at my mouth to remove any sign that I'd been kissing her. I hope her perfume didn't rub off on me. I might be sick if I can't get away from that smell. It's not exactly bad, but it's what she always wears, which means the scent sends me right back to my time with her. And I don't want to be there.

Even if it would help me to forget Jane.

"I don't get it. What did I do wrong?"

"You didn't do anything wrong." I straighten my collar and tighten my tie, but I don't look at her. "It's just not a good idea."

Wrong thing to say. Then again, I'm not sure there'd be any good thing to say right now. Her dark eyes flash fire. "Are you kidding me? What the hell is wrong with you?"

I wish I knew. I would tell her if I could and if it would get her to shut up. She's attracting attention, which means I'm attracting attention. And I don't want to do that. Not when my father is finally looking at me with something other than disdain.

"This is wrong. That's all. Why can't you grow up and let it go?" I snap.

Her face goes a shade of red I've never seen a face turn before. Not even Dad's when he's really mad at me.

"*I'm* the one who needs to grow up? You're the fucking child who doesn't know what he wants! You think you can flirt with me and do whatever you want to me, then turn around and tell me it's *wrong*?"

And all of a sudden, I know how Jane felt. She got into something she didn't necessarily think through, and freaked out when it went further than she could handle. And I was blaming her all this time. I might not have admitted in my head that I thought she was a tease, but I definitely thought it way down deep. I never figured out that it wasn't about me or what she did to me. It was about her.

And I need to know what it is, because she means too much to me to just walk away.

And that scares the shit out of me.

"This has nothing to do with you." I sigh and run my fingers through my hair. "When will you get it through your head that not everything has to do with you? You're not the center of the damn universe."

I glance around the room and wish everybody

would find something else to pay attention to. Okay, so maybe I'm being too harsh on her, since it's not her fault that I can't stop thinking about Jane. And it's not really Trinity's fault that she thinks things with us might be getting going again. I made the first move. It was on me.

"Really, Anthony? That's the fucking best you've got?" She throws back another shot. "I seem to remember you thinking my pussy was the center of the universe. You couldn't get enough of it."

Shit.

This is not how things were supposed to go down.

I look around to try to figure out how to best diffuse things. Trinity's waving for another drink, and everyone's looking at us. I need to nip this in the bud or it's going to end up going viral and all the good will my dad has toward me will go out the window. And that's the best-case scenario. The worst case is Chambersmith finding out and me losing the account on top of everything else.

I'm seriously considering picking her up and throwing her over my shoulder when my wing man finally decides to act like a wing man.

"Trinity, come on." Tyler puts her coat over her shoulders and leads her to the door. Well, drags her is more like it. She practically kicks and screams the entire way, hurling curses at me as she does.

I deserve a few of them. Maybe not all, but a lot.

"Here you go." A waitress hands me a drink. "You look like you could use it."

I take it gladly and take a seat, running my hands

through my hair to smooth it down. I did the right thing. We're no good together. Everybody seems to have forgotten the scene we made as soon as it's over, too, so the night is turning around. The last thing I need is for Dad to decide I can't be trusted with the Chambersmith account.

How is it possible for a single woman to turn me into somebody I don't recognize? This isn't me at all, the guy who cares about feelings and doing the right thing. Not that I ever deliberately did the wrong thing. Well, it's rarely deliberate. I am human after all. More often, I just never thought about whether what I did was right. Now, I'd give anything to have Jane here so I could apologize for not trying harder to understand why she ran away.

"Anthony!"

My head snaps around in the direction of the door, and I stop just short of rubbing my eyes to make sure I'm not dreaming. There she is, marching over to me. I can't decide if she's happy or angry or what, but it doesn't matter right now. She's here. It feels like I haven't seen her in years. My heart does some weird trippy thing.

"Jane?" I barely have time to say her name before she takes me by the lapels of my jacket and pulls me to her for a kiss better than anything Trinity or any other girl has ever given. The best kiss of my life. I slide my arms around her waist to hold her, not to pull her to me, necessarily, just to touch her. It's enough just to touch her.

Her lips are like silk, and her taste...fuck, how did

I forget that taste? All I want is more, but I know this isn't the time or the place. Especially since the only thing worse than getting caught arguing with Trinity in public is having someone publish that I was making out with two different women within minutes of each other.

When I step back, we're both out of breath.

"I'm ready now," she whispers. "Come on. Let's get out of here."

"You're sure?" Every nerve in my body is screaming for me to take her up on it, but I can't risk her running off again. She's worth more than a quick fuck. Or even a long leisurely one if it means that's all I get. "I don't want you to feel like you have to."

She nods, her eyes shining. "Stop overthinking it."

CHAPTER TWENTY-ONE
JANE

When I see him at the club, in that moment before he turns and sees me, he has such a lost expression on his face that it breaks my heart. And it helps me make my decision. I don't want to be scared anymore. I want to do this, and not just because I know he wants it, but because *I* want it.

Then he looks at me and the heat in his gaze is enough to send desire rocketing through me.

I'm walking toward him with only one thought on my mind: I need to touch him.

The kiss is everything I hoped it would be. It's intentional on both parts, and for the right reasons this time. There's no wondering why or what the other person's thinking.

When he asks me if I'm sure, I know I've made the right choice. He barely takes his eyes off me as he tells a friend that he's leaving. He just nods at Chloe, but out of the corner of my eye, I see her beaming. I tell myself I need to thank her, but there will be time for that later.

There's a town car waiting when we leave the club, and I expect Anthony to give the driver his address as soon as he slides in next to me. Instead, he asks, "Will you be more comfortable at your place or mine?"

"I think we'll both be more comfortable at yours," I say. "My bed is that futon, remember?"

He gives me a wry sort of smile as he brushes back some hair from my face. "Sadly, I don't really remember much, but I'll take your word for it." He wraps a lock of hair around his finger. "I don't want you to feel any pressure. If you want me to stop at any point—"

"You will, I know." I take his hand and press a kiss to his palm.

"I don't want to jinx this, but can I ask what made you change your mind?" He laces his fingers between mine and rests our hands on his knee.

I know I'll need to tell him about my past, but this isn't the right moment. So I give him the truth, but not all of it. "Chloe talked some sense into me." He raises an eyebrow, and I add, "She reminded me that I can trust you."

The rest of the ride to his place is quiet. He keeps me close, tucked under his arm, our hands clasped together. I wait for the panic to kick in, for the memories to come pouring forward. I'm in a car. With a man. Who's touching me.

When nothing happens, I force myself to think of each specific thing. Better to work on calming myself now and have it all under control by the time we get to his place, than to freak out right before we take that last step like I did before.

The flashbacks don't come. My uncle's face stays in the past. It's only Anthony's hands. His scent. The warmth of his body.

For the first time since it happened, I feel like I'm in control of every part of me.

We maintain our silence until we reach his door, but the air between us is steadily thickening. My heart is loud in my ears, my body warming as my stomach twists and churns. He won't hurt me. He would never. He only wants to bring me pleasure. Be with me.

He leads me to the bedroom, taking me in his arms as he kicks the door closed behind us. I expect a fast, deep kiss, one that takes us right back to the place we were before I freaked out on him, but his lips are gentle against mine. He lets the fire between us gradually build as he traces my bottom lip with his tongue. I open my mouth as I push myself on my tiptoes, my arms winding around his neck. I can feel his erection pushing against my stomach, and my pussy clenches in reaction.

"Anthony," I moan his name as he moves from his slow exploration of my mouth to planting soft kisses down my jaw, and then down my throat.

I'm barely aware that he's undressing me until I'm down to my panties and bra and the heat of his hands is scorching my skin. Then it's all about getting him naked, and my fingers shake as I tug at the bottom of his shirt. He takes a step back and pulls it over his head. I trace his muscles with my fingertips, feeling them jump at each pass. His body is a true work of art.

I go for his jeans next. I didn't get a chance to see him before, and the need is almost too much. I go to my knees to help him from his jeans, then realize that I'm at a good place to try something new, something I never imagined I'd want to do. When I reach for the waist of his underwear, he sucks in a breath, but doesn't stop me.

I swallow hard as I see him for the first time. Thick and arching up toward his stomach, he's even bigger than I thought. For the first time, I'm grateful that those gymnastic classes at the Y when I was a kid had taken care of my hymen. Things are probably going to be a bit uncomfortable even without that added issue.

"You don't have to—"

"Do you want me to?" I cut off his statement with a question.

He shudders and reaches down to run his thumb along my bottom lip. "Fuck, yes, Jane. But only if you—"

Whatever else he planned to say is lost in a strangled groan as I take the tip of him into my mouth. I can only get a couple inches, but based on the curses I'm hearing, I feel confident that he's enjoying what I'm doing. I may be a virgin, but I grew up with a lot of kids who weren't, and when there's two or three girls in a single room, information is shared.

Information that I'm currently putting to the test as I circle his tip with my tongue, stroke the base of his shaft with one free hand while the other moves a bit lower. He puts his hand in my hair and his hips move forward, sliding a bit more of his cock into my mouth. The skin is impossibly smooth against my tongue, the flesh beneath it hard.

"Jane, sweetheart." His voice is rough as he takes a step back. "Too much."

For a moment, I try to follow him, wanting to feel him come in my mouth, but then I remember that there's something else I want more.

He takes my shoulders and pulls me to my feet. I'm not there long as he eases me back on his bed. He leans over me, his mouth covering mine in a deep kiss as his hands rid me of my bra and then my panties. When he finally straightens, his eyes slide down my body, and I fist my hands in the blankets to keep from covering myself.

"Do you have any idea how gorgeous you are?" His fingers curl around my ankles, spreading my legs so that he can kneel between them.

The compliment sounds like a line, but I know it's not. I can read the sincerity in his eyes. He truly thinks I'm beautiful.

It's on the tip of my tongue to share one of my two secrets: the one that's a bit more relevant to the current situation. But then his mouth closes over my nipple, and all thoughts flee.

I arch my back to encourage him, pushing myself into him, holding the back of his neck to pull him closer. I cry out his name as his teeth lightly scrape the tight flesh, then curse when he takes the tip between his teeth and tugs. My eyes flutter closed when he starts to suck.

His hand slides between my thighs to stroke me, and I almost see stars when his fingers press against my throbbing, aching flesh. His thumb passes over my clit as a finger slips inside. This time, all I feel is the pleasure that comes with each stroke. The past stays where it belongs and leaves me with him.

"So sweet," he whispers as he works his way further down my body, a second finger joining the first. "So tight."

My hips move, rolling in circles, as he drives me crazy with his fingers, his thumb. His mouth. His tongue laps at the sensitive skin between my thighs, and I whimper. It's too much, sensory overload, the way my body screams for more combined with his own moans. Knowing I'm turning him on just adds to my own arousal.

I arch again as I come, shivering and shuddering. I let go and let myself fly, knowing he'll be here to catch me when I come down. It's pure bliss.

When I come to, he's making little patterns on my stomach with his fingers. I reach for him, skimming his taut, chiseled body, learning all the little dips and planes. He's beautiful, perfect, and he wants me. Me! It's the most incredible feeling, just knowing that the thick, long dick he rolls a condom down is hard because of me. I hold my arms out to him and welcome his weight as he lowers himself over top of me.

He waits, looking down into my eyes. "Are you sure?" he asks, his voice softer than I've ever heard it. He's shaking with the strain of holding back, and yet he's still taking the time to ask me that. That's all I need to tell me that I've made the right choice.

"Yes."

I've never been more sure of anything in my life. When the pressure gets stronger, I do my best to relax as he eases his way inside. I don't regret any of this, not one bit, even as the discomfort rounds the corner into pain and I can't stop the gasp. While I hate the circumstances that led to my remaining a virgin, I'm glad I waited for him instead of having some awkward tumble in the backseat of a car with some random guy. He prepared me well, and it doesn't take more than a few seconds for nature to do its work, slicking the place where the two of us are joined.

"You okay?" he murmurs, the question strained.

I nod wordlessly. I can't speak. Tears sting behind my eyes, but they're not tears of pain. There's so much happening in my head and my heart, I can't focus on just one thought or one feeling. I wonder if he feels it, too. If he understands just how much this moment means to me. Not because I have some naive romantic notions linked to my first time, but because he's taken care of me so well.

He's right above me, his lips skimming my forehead and cheeks and throat. I tilt my head back and he presses his face into the curve of my throat, his breath hot against my skin, but it's a good heat, just like the pressure deep in my core as he begins to move is a good pressure, sweet and right. So right.

The whole thing is right. The way his body rests on top of mine, and the way I raise my hips to meet his steady strokes. I don't even have to think about it.

It's instinct, deep and natural and ancient. Even that initial pain is part of it, though it's since faded under the sweetness that comes with every perfectly angled thrust.

I run my hands up and down his back, grip his firm ass, and kiss his shoulder. I close my eyes, sinking into the sensations, letting the heat building between us carry me away to that place beyond thought or reason.

I moan, my breath coming in short little gasps as I near the edge again. He pulls back so that our eyes can meet, and I see so many emotions swirling there that I can't name them all. Sliding his arms under my shoulders, he holds me closer. I wrap mine around his neck, my legs tightening around his waist, not a sliver of space between us. We're together, our bodies joined as one, riding the waves of pleasure that are building and growing. He speeds up, and his breath comes faster, harder, more ragged.

"Yes…yes…Anthony, yes...!"

I'm going to come again, and this time, he's coming with me, driving himself into me with hard, fast strokes. He grunts and pants like an animal, and I want him to, I want all of him. I scream into his neck as my body convulses underneath him. His cries ring in my ears, and I clutch him as hard as I can.

I hold him close as we float, then slowly descend back into reality. Even though he doesn't know about my past, and doesn't know that he's my first, I feel like being with him washed clean everything that my uncle sullied. Now, when I feel the ghost of a touch, it will be Anthony's. It will be his face I see. His scent and his body.

He pushes himself up a little and slides out of me. I feel a sense of loss I can't explain, like he's leaving. Only he's not leaving. He rolls onto his back and pulls me close, wrapping me in his strong arms where the aftershocks make me shiver.

"Are you all right?" He skims his fingers over my arm in a soothing gesture that warms me more than any blanket could have.

I rest my head on his chest, knowing that I still need to tell him my secrets. But not yet. Soon. But not now. "I'm great," I answer honestly. "When can we do it again?"

CHAPTER TWENTY-TWO
ANTHONY

"I don't think two weeks have ever passed as fast as these two." I shake my head as I rearrange the notes for the presentation. I should have these all memorized by now, seeing as I've been through them dozens of times.

"Two weeks haven't passed," Jane reminds me with one of her patented wry smiles. Her eyes dance. "It's only been ten days."

"Cute." I have to smile, because she is cute. More than cute. Beautiful and sexy and smart and sweet... she's everything.

It's amazing that we've been able to get any work done at all, really. We're in that amazing bubble a couple lives in during the early days of a relationship. And it is a relationship, much to my surprise. Even more shocking is that it doesn't freak me out to use the 'r' word.

When we're not having sex, we're sleeping in between sessions or making out or talking on the phone when we can't be together. And, somehow, in the middle of it all, we've put together a killer presentation. A lot of it, I know, has to do with the fact that Jane multi-tasks during sex, and I don't mean that just because she does things with her mouth *and* hands that should be illegal. She actually likes to brainstorm for ideas while we're cuddling. Or, not *cuddling*, because I don't do that. I'm sure there's a more manly word for it. Whatever it's called, I've gotten more done in the time I'm with her than I normally get done in weeks. Maybe months.

And what we're coming up with is really, really good. I keep asking myself if I'm not being just a little overly optimistic, but every time I look at the ideas Jane and I have come up with together, I can't help but feel proud. I couldn't do any of this without her, and I know it. What's more, so does she. But she needs me, too. We need each other, and that's something completely new for both of us.

It's strange that we grew up in two totally different worlds, but there's still so much we have in common. A feeling that it's us against the world. Loneliness even when we're surrounded by people. Wearing a mask.

I know there are things she's hiding. I can see it on her face and in her eyes that she wants to tell me but can't. Not yet. My gut tells me that at least one of those things is the reason why that first night ended with her running away. But as much as I want to know, I want to prove to her that she can trust me.

"Where should the stats go?" she asks from where she's creating charts of competitor sales. "I mean, there's an argument for putting them in the beginning of the presentation, just to get them out of the way, but there's also one for putting them in the middle and opening with something really strong to catch their attention, reel them in."

"Let's go with the middle and run through the presentation that way. We'll see how it feels."

It's bizarre, working on an actual presentation, molding the ideas we come up with together, turning them into something better than I ever could've imagined. I feel like a real, honest-to-God ad man. Me. The guy who used to swear I wanted nothing to do with Dad's business. I'm actually good at it.

"Where do you want to do dinner tonight?" I ask when my stomach rumbles.

She pouts as she turns. "We're taking time out for dinner?" She reaches out and toys with one of my buttons.

Another appetite roars to life within me. "You're insatiable."

"It's all your fault." She stretches up and plants a soft kiss on my waiting lips. Even that little bit of contact is electric, but it doesn't keep me from seeing the hint of a shadow that crosses her face.

One of those secrets.

I don't call her on it, though.

"I hate to spoil things for you, but I need to eat if you want me to have any energy. Sorry." I toss her a wink and dedicate myself to finishing for the day so we can get the hell out of the office. And into a bed.

Now that she has me thinking along carnal lines, I can't think about anything else but being inside her, feeling her underneath me, above me. Fuck. I have it bad.

"To answer your question, it doesn't matter where we go for dinner. You know me. I'm pretty simple when it comes to things like that." Her smile is warm and genuine. "I'm just happy to be with you. Happier than, well, than I can remember ever being."

I wish I could explain to her how she makes me feel when she says things like that. Like a king. Just the thought that I could make a woman like her happy is unreal. She's turning me into a better person just by being with me because I want to be better for her.

"You don't want to go to some big, fancy place?" I joke. "What's the point of sleeping with the boss if you don't take advantage by going out for expensive dinners?"

Her laugh reminds me of the sound of bells. "Please. I wouldn't know what to do with myself in a big, fancy place. Or even a small, fancy place. I could hardly handle eating dinner in your apartment that first night." She flushes.

That gives me pause, but not because I remember what happened after dinner. I look up from my laptop. She's sitting on the sofa against the wall, working on her own laptop.

"Hang on a sec. Does it make you uncomfortable going to places like that with me?" I get up and cross over to her. "I'm used to it. I barely even notice it anymore. I didn't think about your feelings."

She blushes. "That's sweet."

I raise an eyebrow. "That I didn't think about your

feelings?"

"That you even thought to ask me at all, dope." She shakes her head with a giggle. "I love life here. I love what we're doing together. Working with you, I feel like a kick-ass career woman in a rom-com or TV show." She pauses, then adds, "But really? I sort of miss the simpler life."

I smile at the confession. "You mean the way you grew up?"

"Yeah, but minus the foster home."

Another of those shadows crosses her face, vanishing a bit slower this time.

"Country life. I miss that." Her expression grows wistful. "Or maybe I just miss what I always thought it could be. Quiet mornings, the smell of coffee in the kitchen. Taking a cup out to the front porch and watching the sun rise. Watching fireflies at night in the summer. Knowing the neighbors. That kind of thing. Everything's so crazy, but so isolated at the same time here, you know? So many more people, but so much less connection."

She never ceases to amaze me. She's not only deeper and kinder than any woman I've ever known. She manages to make small-town life look appealing, something I never would've imagined possible before meeting her. Just another way she makes me a better man.

I reach for her hand and pull her up hard enough for her to crash against my chest. "Forget eating out. We'll order in."

With our eyes locked together, I reach down and

slide my hand between her legs. The door's closed, but we're both aware of how easily someone could come in. She doesn't stop me, though. Instead, she lets out a little moan and rocks her hips forward, a clear encouragement.

I move my hand higher, then stare down at her in shock as I meet bare flesh. Her cheeks are stained red.

"Are you trying to kill me, Jane?" My voice is hoarse. My cock presses painfully against my zipper.

She bites her bottom lip and peers up at me through her lashes. "I thought you said you were hungry."

Fuck.

Who the hell taught this woman to be so damn innocent and seductive all at once?

I can't get enough of her. She's right outside my office door and somehow I'm even more aware of her today than I was yesterday. Part of that could be because now every time I look at my desk, all I can picture is how last night I picked her up and put her on my desk, then dropped to my knees and made her scream.

Sort of.

We were at work, so I couldn't actually make her scream, but I ate her out for at least a half hour and gave her five orgasms, so I feel pretty confident that she would've been screaming if she hadn't bit down on the side of her hand.

I wonder if she's thinking of it, too. If the faint marks on her hand remind her of what it was like to have my face buried in her pussy, her hand in my hair, egging me on.

Dammit.

I'm rock hard, and there's no relief in sight.

She's so close, but so far. We weren't far apart earlier this morning in the shower. I smile a little at the memory of our soapy bodies sliding against each other as I picked her up and took her against the wall.

Yeah, that's not really helping the whole erection problem I have right now.

A brisk knock at the door stirs me back to reality, and I wave in the random clerk who hands me an interoffice envelope. It's a good thing I wait until I'm alone to open it because the envelope holds only one thing: a pair of panties I remember watching Jane slide into earlier.

I reach down and adjust myself and take all of thirty seconds to consider the possible ramifications of what I want to do before hitting the intercom button.

"Miss Ward, I have a situation here that needs your immediate attention."

Judging by the smirk on her face when she comes in, she knows exactly what the situation is. She closes the door, turns the lock, and then makes her way across the office.

"Where do you want me?" she asks. "On my knees... or on your lap?"

I somehow know this is going to be the hardest decision I make today.

CHAPTER TWENTY-THREE

JANE

"Are you sure we put the research and stats in the right place?" He's pacing behind his desk the way his father does, hands clasped behind his back. I decide it's better to keep that observation to myself at the moment.

I tried my best to help him relax, but I know how much he has riding on this, so there's only so much I can do. Right now, it's time for some reassurance.

"We've gone over it a million different ways. It's perfect as it is. Everything is exactly how it should be."

Including him. If there's one thing he's good at, it's looking like a million bucks. His suit fits like it was made for him, which I'm sure it was. He definitely plays the part of a self-assured, skilled advertising executive even when I know he's plagued with doubt.

"I'll go first with the big ideas, then you can come in with the facts and figures. I'll close it out. What do you think?" He glances at me as he continues to pace.

"You want me to present with you?" My knees feel watery all of a sudden. Hell. No.

"Why not? This is just as much yours as it is mine." He looks genuinely perplexed by my surprise.

"I don't think so."

It's a terrible idea. He just doesn't see it at the moment. If we were to present together, he wouldn't be able to take full credit for the work. He needs to get the credit if he's ever going to be taken seriously. I'm sure I'll have my time, someday. I didn't do any of this thinking my name would be on it.

"You want me to go in there on my own?"

Suddenly, that little boy I see from time to time is back, and this time it's as much fear as vulnerability that brings him out.

I go to him, smoothing my hands over his lapels before resting them on his chest. A surge of emotion goes through me, strong enough to make something inside me hurt. I haven't said it to him yet, but I've known it since the first time we slept together.

But now's not the time to tell him.

"Yes. That's exactly what I want you to do. This is your baby. Go in there and prove yourself. Not just to them, but to you."

He smiles and his eyes go soft and warm. I like him better this way. "Do me a favor, then," he murmurs, taking me by the waist.

"What's that?"

"Come in with me, at least. You don't have to present, but I would feel a lot better if you were in there."

"Okay. I don't think that would raise any eyebrows." After all, I'm his assistant. It's a little thrilling, too, the thought of watching our work on display. Of seeing all the effort pay off.

He checks his Rolex. On anyone else, the move would seem pretentious, but on him, it's natural. "Okay. Time to go in."

We both take a deep breath and stride out of his office like there's not a worry in the world. I'm so proud of him, and he hasn't even started the presentation yet. As we walk past other James employees, eyes follow us, and a part of me wishes I could tell them all that he's mine.

It's as much my choice as his that we aren't going public yet. Neither of us wants to deal with the stigma of the boss and assistant sleeping together. We want to wait until we're a bit more established. That's the smart thing to do, but it doesn't change the desire to stake my claim. At least when we pass Chloe, she gives me a conspiratorial wink, and I remember that there is at least one person with whom I can be completely honest.

The conference room is full of suits when we arrive. Mr. James is there, too, an expectant look on his face. I recognize the man sitting to his right as well. He reminds me of a weasel, which is probably why his face has made an impression on me. I remember Anthony pointing him out to me a couple days ago. His cousin, Jerrod.

And he hates me. Or, at least, resents my presence in the conference room. He stares as we walk in and Anthony introduces me as his assistant. I can just about feel the waves of displeasure coming from him. Terrific.

Anthony doesn't seem to notice, which is for the best. He has enough on his mind. I have to remind myself over and over not to mouth the presentation along with him as he runs through it. I don't want anyone in here to know how much of a hand I've had in it. The Chambersmith guys might take it as me just having heard the presentation several times, but Mr. James and Jerrod would probably suspect more.

From time to time, I tear my eyes away from Anthony and glance over at Mr. Chambersmith to find him smiling and nodding. I can see he loves our commercial ideas, the social media outreach plan—YouTube ads, Instagram campaigns, the whole nine yards. Together, Anthony and I came up with an entire series of posts that created a story from beginning to end, a series which will ideally influence followers to keep up with the story's progression. Something to tug at the heartstrings while selling lots and lots of stationery.

By the time he finishes by throwing out competitor numbers and their history in the markets we're trying to connect with, Mr. Chambersmith is about ready to jump out of his chair. I can tell he wants to get started immediately, if not sooner. Mr. James, meanwhile, is trying as hard as he can to keep from beaming with pride. Jerrod looks like someone ruined Christmas, Santa Claus, and his birthday all at once.

And Anthony. He shines like the sun. He's in his element at the head of the table, commanding an entire room like he was born to do it. I can't deny that it's a major turn on. Then again, I find pretty much everything about Anthony a turn on. In less than two weeks, I've gone from virgin to sex fiend.

Mr. Chambersmith stands, holding out a hand for Anthony to shake. "Young man, I'm impressed with you. I think I speak for all of us when I say that, too."

"That's a yes, then?" Anthony asks with a dazzling smile.

"Show me the contract, son." They shake hands and the rest of the room, including me, breaks out into applause. Well, everyone except Jerrod. He looks like he'd rather swallow glass than congratulate his cousin. But no one's looking at him. All the attention is on Anthony.

I slide a copy of the contract out from the folder in my lap and pass it across the table. My hands shake a little as I do. There are some pretty big numbers involved, in the multi-millions. Chambersmith signs like he's signing a check in a restaurant.

Oh, to have money like that.

I look up and my eyes meet Anthony's. I know the satisfaction in them is reflected in mine. He did it.

CHAPTER TWENTY-FOUR
ANTHONY

I slap a porterhouse down on the grill and listen to it sizzle. It's got to be one of the most satisfying sounds in life, I think. Up there with a great call for my team in hockey and hearing Jane moan my name. I'm not usually the guy to eat a porterhouse—too much cholesterol, that sort of thing—but I'm in the mood for meat. Something juicy. I'm victorious and really proud of myself for the first time in a long time.

I'm also in my jockey shorts after a long and rather intense make-out session in my room which only came to an end when our stomachs rumbled. Jane ties an apron around my waist to keep me from getting hit with grease spatter, then kisses my bare shoulder. She moves around to my side and lifts a wine glass to my lips as I flip the vegetables sitting on the grill next to the beef. I savor the rich, full-bodied red wine almost as much as the taste of her mouth on mine. Maybe later I'll taste them both at the same time.

“You’re incredible, you know that?” she whispers. Her eyes meet mine and the way they smolder just about undoes me. She’s in her underwear, one of my tailored shirts hanging open on her tiny frame so I can see hints of cleavage and red lace. She looks fragile and unbearably sexy all at once. The fragile bit is just appearance. I know all too well how strong she is. I remember taking strength from her during the meeting. Just knowing she was there, watching and supporting me, made all the difference. She’s the best thing to ever happen to me. My hands find her body even though they should really be taking care of dinner.

The food doesn’t seem that important as I take her mouth. My tongue slips between her lips, and I learn that the combination of the wine and her is indeed as heady as I expected. I’ll have to try it on some other body parts.

I lift her onto the island across from the stove and relish the tightening of her legs around my waist as the kiss deepens. She’s just as eager for me as I am for her, and the knowledge that a woman this amazing wants me makes me feel more powerful than anything I’ve ever done.

Her fingers tangle in my hair, then work on the knot she just tied to undo the apron. As it falls to the floor, she presses her face against my bare chest, raining kisses across my skin. When her teeth worry at my nipple, I groan. I smell the steak burning just before burying my face between her breasts and inhaling a much sweeter scent.

She’s like a fucking drug. I can’t get enough of her.

She groans, holding my head to her breasts as I began to lick and bite my way across her flesh until I find one tight nipple. She wriggles against me, rubbing my thickening dick against the crotch of her increasingly wet panties, and soon we're humping through our underwear, breathless, hands and mouths all over each other. I suck on her nipple harder this time, and her back arches as she groans in satisfaction.

"Screw this," I mutter as I lift her in my arms.

A quick flick of the wrist turns off the stove. Not in time to save our food, but at least preventing a fire. A lost dinner is one thing. I don't feel like having the fire department interrupt my night. I can afford to replace some steak and vegetables.

I carry her to the bedroom and throw her onto the bed. She squeals softly, giggling, but that giggle dies when she feels my hands gliding up from ankle to thigh. I peel off her panties and waste no time getting a condom ready. We've done enough foreplay, and the dark look on her face tells me she agrees. I'm rock hard by the time I settle between her legs.

Just before I slide into her, she puts her hands on my chest. I give her a puzzled look until she gives me a little push. I grin as I grab her waist and spin us around so she's on top of me.

"Let me do the work," she whispers against my lips.

Then she pushes herself up on her knees, letting my shirt fall open to expose those gorgeous breasts of hers. She reaches underneath her and wraps her fist around my cock. I start to groan, but it turns into a curse as she begins to lower herself onto me.

"Anthony, fuck. Oh, fuck!" Her curses are almost as sweet as the sensation of sliding into that tight sheath.

So tight.

Her eyes are closed by the time she's taken all of me, her palms flat on my stomach, nails biting into my skin. I love watching her like this, how she abandons all pretenses, drops all of her walls and inhibitions. I reach up and palm her breasts, kneading them, teasing her nipples between finger and thumb. She rides me fast and hard, her pussy squeezing me as I feel her thigh muscles flexing against my waist.

I can feel myself closing in on my release, and I know she's not quite there yet, so I drop one of my hands and press my thumb against her clit. I make quick back and forth movements, taking her to the edge as fast as she's taking me. I still get there first, white-hot pleasure coursing through me. But she follows a few seconds later, collapsing onto me as she cries out my name. I wrap my arms around her and hold her tight.

I don't like the idea of letting her go.

As we lie there, she shifts off of me, but keeps pressed against my side.

"Can I tell you something?"

Her voice is small, and I wonder if I'm going to finally hear one of those things that make the shadows go across her face.

"Have you ever had a secret so deep that you want to tell someone, but you're terrified that people will look at you differently when they find out?"

I kiss the top of her head and stroke my hand down her bare arm. "I will never look at you any differently, no matter what you tell me. You can trust me."

She takes a deep breath, but I don't push her. When she starts to talk, it takes everything in me to stay calm when all I want to do is find that fucking *bastard* and chop his balls off. Then feed them to him. While he's tied to a fire ant hill. Covered in honey. Naked. In hundred and twenty-degree heat.

All of this is running through my head, but I don't share any of it with her, because that's not what she needs right now. What she needs is for me to tighten my arms around her, kiss her, tell her that it doesn't change the way I feel about her. I can't quite bring myself to say the *l* word yet, but as her body relaxes, I know she understands.

I stay awake until she falls asleep, and only then do I let myself do it as well.

It's dark when I wake up the next morning. I can't stand winter mornings. I like waking up to sun, but that's just not possible when I have a job to get to. I don't think Dad would care very much if I told him I prefer getting out of bed after the sun's high in the sky. I reach for her without thinking twice. Maybe she'll be up for another go-round before we get out of bed. Or we could take a shower together. That's always fun.

Except she's not there.

My eyes fly open when I realize I'm touching empty bed beside me. I listen hard, but can't hear any noise coming from the bathroom. The kitchen, maybe? It would be just like her to fix breakfast for me. I tie the belt of my robe loosely around my waist before going out to greet her. Maybe we'll get through an entire meal together without groping at each other, even though that doesn't sound very fun to me.

She's sitting at the island with her back to me, reading something on her laptop. "You know, you don't have to prove to me that you're a hard worker," I mumble as I enter the kitchen. "I'm not your boss right now, remember?"

She doesn't answer. She doesn't even look at me when my voice breaks the silence.

"Babe? What's wrong?" I'm still rubbing sleep out of my eyes as I walk over to her. She still doesn't look at me. I wonder if she heard me, but I know she had to. I'm standing barely two feet away.

It's only when I'm close enough to look over her shoulder that I see what she's staring at, and it all makes sense. My stomach sinks like it's turned to lead. Fucking parasite paparazzi. Who the hell was taking pictures in the club? And who the hell would think that's even a story?

Above a picture of me and a woman who looks a hell of a lot like Trinity is a headline: *On Again?* Judging from the way we're sucking each other's faces off, it sure looks like we're on again.

I wish I could strangle whoever took the picture. Soulless vultures. I wish they'd stay the hell away from my life.

"What is this?" Jane's voice is little more than a whisper. I open my mouth to assure her it means nothing, to try to explain what looks inexplicable. Only I have no voice. Nothing comes out because, really, there's nothing I can say that'll help. I look guilty. I feel that way, too.

Especially since it's not like Trinity was forcing herself on me. I may have stopped her eventually, but I was a willing participant.

Jane turns to me, and the lack of light in her eyes twists a knife in my chest.

"What the *hell* is this?" she asks again.

CHAPTER TWENTY-FIVE
JANE

My chin trembles, but I hold back just short of letting the tears fall. I won't let him see me break down. He doesn't deserve it, and he sure as hell isn't worth it. I put everything out there for him. Told him my darkest, most personal secret...and then I find *this*.

His jaw is slack. Of course it is. He doesn't know what to say because I have him cornered. For once, he can't charm his way out of something. The thought makes me hate him. I hate him for making a fool out of me, for making me regret giving him something so important to me. Not just my virginity, either. My trust and my faith and my heart.

What's worse is that I know better.

"If you can't tell me what it is, can you tell me when it was?" I ask, jerking my thumb in the direction of the laptop screen and that vile, nasty picture with its terrible headline.

Part of me is hoping that he'll say the picture is from months ago, before we met. If that's all it is, I'll have my own issues feeling insecure about how gorgeous that woman is, but that's completely different than if it's more recent. My gut tells me that's not the case, though.

"I know it's the club you go to all the time because I recognize it. I found you there that one night, the night we..." I can't make myself finish. I'm not sure I want to remember sleeping with him that first time.

He nods as he runs a hand over his tousled hair, then over the stubble that covers his chiseled jaw. Normally I find all of that sexy. Not this morning.

"Yeah. Yeah, it was the club." He pauses, takes a deep breath, and adds, "It was that night, too. The same night."

My heart shatters, and so does my relative calm. "You were with her that same night? What, before I got there? Did she shut you down? Is that why you kissed me back? Is that why you—"

I can't say it, but I also can't keep myself from thinking it. Thinking that maybe he didn't choose to be with me because he cares about me. I'm just...*easy*.

His eyes fly open wide. "Hey! I didn't go looking for you that night. You came there looking for me. It's not like I was trolling around."

I stare at him, unable to believe that things are falling apart so fast. "You're defending yourself?"

"I shouldn't have to, for fuck's sake!" he practically shouts. "You walked away from *me,* remember? You said we should forget what happened between us. So that's what I was trying to do! Forget! Dammit, Jane!"

He's right about that. I'd been the one who ended things before they really got started.

"Don't forget, Jane, you're the one who ran off and wouldn't acknowledge me for days. I didn't know what you were thinking, or if you would ever even set foot in the office again!"

"So, you just found some random girl to make out with?"

"She's my ex," he admits. "All right? It didn't mean anything. I was miserable and trying to forget, and she was there. Besides, you and I weren't together yet. This was before—"

"Before I walked in and kissed you," I finish for him, my voice is flat, devoid of emotion. "But it meant nothing, right? Just like she meant nothing."

"Come on, Jane..."

"No, Anthony. You pushed her off your lap to make room for me. It's how you are. It's how you've always been. Don't think I never heard rumors about your social life." My hands are shaking, but my voice is still steady. "I was interchangeable. Just another body in the long line of women you've gone through. I wasn't the first, and I won't be the last."

"You have no right to say that. My past has nothing to do with this." He's deadly calm now, his voice like ice. "You of all people should know that what's in a person's past shouldn't be held against him."

"I *trusted* you," I whisper. I thought nothing he said could break me more than I already was. Now I know better.

His shoulders fall. "Jane, I didn't mean...let's not do this. Don't you see what's happening? Things were going so well, but here we are, letting something stupid get in between us."

"You think it's stupid? My feelings are stupid?"

"You know that's not what I mean! Why do you insist on twisting my words around?" He points to the laptop, still sitting there between us. "What happened between Trinity and me means nothing. It's stupid. A huge mistake. And we're better than this."

I shake my head and stand. "We're nothing, Anthony. If what you felt for me was real at all, you wouldn't have been able to go back to her like that. I know that it's my fault for running away and hiding, for not telling you what was wrong. I thought it didn't matter when you didn't come after me, because when I came to you, you kissed me back. But it matters now."

"Why? Why does it matter now when it didn't before?"

I can't look at him. "Because now I know that you didn't come after me because you already had someone."

Tears fill my eyes and this time, I don't bother trying to hold them back. I was afraid to give someone my heart, but I took a chance on him. And he's destroyed me.

"What that picture doesn't show is that I stopped it. I told her that it wasn't going to work." He takes a step toward me, and I fold my arms across my chest. "And that's because of you. I couldn't be with her because I didn't want anyone but you. I *don't* want anyone but you."

I want to believe him. To brush it all aside and go back to the happy place, but the bubble's burst and reality is back. A reality where a poor orphan from rural Pennsylvania can never be with her billionaire CEO boss.

"You only think you want me." The words are quiet, but I know he can hear me because I see him stiffen. "I'm something different. New. And pretty soon, you'll get bored, and you'll want to go back to your old life."

"I won't," he insists.

My smile is sad. "But you already did. As soon as things got tough, you went straight back to your ex. It wasn't cheating, I know that, but you didn't fight then, and you won't fight in the future." I swallow hard. "It's better this way."

He looks aghast. "But I love you."

Tears roll down my cheeks. Nobody's ever said that to me before. Damn him for saying it now.

"I don't believe you," I say in a voice choked with tears. Before he can add anything else, I continue, "I quit. I never want to see you or speak to you again."

And I mean it. Every word. My heart won't be able to handle it if I do anything else.

CHAPTER TWENTY-SIX
ANTHONY

I have no choice but to go to work. I just signed a multi-million-dollar deal, and I'm now legally bound to see it through. Nobody bothers to tell you there's another side to success. When you finally score big, people expect you to keep doing it. You can't crawl into bed and pull the blankets over your head the day after you bluffed your way into a big ad campaign just because you got dumped.

No, I didn't bluff my way in. I knew what I was talking about. I just needed a lot of help. And now she's gone. From my work and my bed and my life. She'll never come back, not after everything she said.

My heart is heavy as my driver opens the car door for me. I usually enjoy the luxury of a chauffeured town car, but I can't even muster up the strength to care. All the money in the world and I couldn't care less without her.

There's one comfort: nobody at work knows what

happened. Jane and I kept things quiet about us, so the only person who knows about that is Chloe. Everyone else only knows I scored big yesterday. And since I made it clear in the past that I didn't want an assistant, I'm sure no one will be surprised when Jane doesn't show up.

They smile when they see me step off the elevator and nod and congratulate me and tell me what a good job I did. Kiss ups, sure, but it still feels good to hear it. At least the entire world doesn't think I'm a faithless, heartless loser. It doesn't make it feel any less hollow, though.

I'll forget her. I'll have to. At least there won't be any time to brood when I have a campaign to head. I ignore the sick feeling in my stomach when I think about doing it without her. I can do this.

My chair is barely warm when Dad calls in on my speaker phone. "I want to see you, now," he barks.

"Good morning to you, too," I mutter under my breath as I stand, buttoning my suit jacket, and smoothing a hand back over my hair to make sure it's in place. Why do I even care what he thinks about the way I look? Regardless, it's a habit. I hope he doesn't want to talk for too long. I'll probably beg off, tell him I'm busy, then lock the door and sit by myself all day. I can't imagine concentrating enough to get anything done.

Dad's sitting with his back to me when I get to his office. Funny, seeing as how he called me, but it's a power play. Everything with him is a power play.

I knock on the open door. "You wanted to see me?"

"Close the door."

And here I am, thinking he was calling me to congratulate me again for yesterday. His voice is so cold, I'm surprised the windows aren't frosted over. This is going to be fun. Once he hears the latch turn, he turns in his chair. It's official. His face is roughly the same shade as an eggplant.

Fuck.

I sigh. "What did I do this time?" Might as well get it over with. I stand with my hands clasped behind my back and wait for the storm to rage, then blow over.

This isn't one of the usual storms, however. I can tell when he doesn't stand up. He normally does that when he wants to stare me down. Instead, he leans his elbows on the arms of his chair and tents his fingers beneath his chin.

"I want to preface what I'm about to say by stating that I don't approve of sneaking around."

"Okay…" Where could this possibly be going? Usually, he's yelling at me for not being subtle enough.

"However," he continues, "when it's in the best interest of my company, not to mention my employees and their livelihoods, I feel it's warranted."

"That's…good to hear," I reply, still waiting for the bomb to drop.

Then, it does. "What the hell were you thinking, using that girl's ideas and calling them your own?" he explodes in a voice that practically shakes the windows.

I stare for a moment before I can even react. "What? Who told you that? How would they even—?" Before he can reply, I figure it all out. "Jerrod? That sneaky son of a bitch!"

"He accessed your email—"

"You mean broke into!"

"I mean accessed!" Dad roars. "It's my damn company! And he saw that she gave you all those ideas! He saw everything!"

I've never liked Jerrod. It's been his mission in life for years to take me down, but never more than when I took the job with Dad. And there've been times I've wanted to knock the daylights out of him, but this is the first time I feel like I actually might lose control if I hit him now.

"Do you even understand what you've done?" Dad asks. "Do you know how much trouble this could make for us? You used her ideas when you know damn well she's not contracted to do that kind of work. She's an intern, for God's sake! Using her intellectual property under false pretenses could leave us open to a lawsuit!"

I have to admit, that gets through to me. I had no idea. I didn't even think that it could be an issue because I never bothered to pay much attention to, well, to anything really.

He's not done yet. "Not only that, but the scandal would ruin my reputation—and my political chances! And for what? So you could pretend to be a big shot?"

"I didn't mean for this to happen."

"Yeah. You never mean for anything to happen, do you?"

I've never heard him sound so hateful before. That's exactly how he sounds, too. Full of hatred. He hates me.

My father *hates* me.

"I'm sorry, son." He doesn't look sorry. Not even a little bit.

"Sorry for what?" I dare ask, though I have a pretty good idea of what's coming. He warned me, after all.

"I gave you one last chance, and you blew it. You have to go."

I feel cold inside. He really wants me gone, just like that. His own son. Okay, so I fucked up. But at least this time I was actually trying to do right.

"It was an honest mistake," I manage to say.

"Bull. You didn't make a mistake. You deliberately used that girl's ideas, just like you use people for everything else you want. You're a screw-up, Anthony, and I can't have that around me, not when there's so much riding on my reputation." He turns away again, facing the window.

The discussion, what there was of it, is officially over. It's not the firing that hurts, not really. If my father wasn't my boss, I probably would have been fired a long time ago. No, no *probably*, about it. I would have been. If it was just that, it wouldn't hurt so much. It's the fact that he's baldly stating what I've always known. His career means more than his son, and that's the real reason I'm being fired. It has little to do with work performance and everything to do with his image.

I have to go. I manage to hold my head high as I walk out of the office, but it doesn't matter. He can't see me, and I admit now that he never has.

CHAPTER TWENTY-SEVEN
ANTHONY

I still keep my head up as I carry the cardboard box with my few possessions from what used to be my office to the elevator. My cheeks burn as I walk past desk after desk, knowing that everyone will know everything, if they don't already. Open office doors reveal people who must've heard Dad's tirade, and they're at least trying to make it look like they're not straining for a look at me as I leave in defeat. Same thing for the heads popping up over the tops of cubicles. And just twenty minutes ago they were congratulating me. Life turns on a dime.

I can't let myself relax until I'm in the elevator with the doors closed. Nobody can see me in there. I don't have to pretend not to care what they think. Normally, I wouldn't. I really wouldn't. But this on top of everything else, it's just too much to smile my way through.

At least my car is waiting for me at the curb. I wouldn't want to wait around on Madison Avenue holding a box full of office supplies, hoping for a cab. I'd be the universal symbol for somebody who just got canned.

"Anthony!" I hear my name and turn to find Chloe rushing to me. "I hoped I would catch you."

I force myself not to snap at her. "What do you want? I'm not really in the mood to talk."

"What if it's about Jane?"

That gets my attention and sends my pulse racing. "What is it?"

"I noticed she didn't come in this morning. I guess she'll never be back."

"No. She quit." I shake my head. "Anyway, it's not like it matters, because she wouldn't have a job now that I'm fired."

Chloe frowns. "She quit? But she loved her job."

"Yeah, well, sometimes things just don't work out, do they?" I can't rehash this with her, and definitely not on the sidewalk.

"Did you do something to screw it up again?"

"Did I?" I can't help but laugh.

Her expression doesn't shift as she puts her hands on her hips. "Yeah. Did you? Because I know how much she cares about you. She wouldn't have quit on you if you hadn't done something to really ruin things."

I sigh. She'd hear it from Jane anyway. "She saw a picture of me and my ex kissing. Some asshole paparazzi snapped it about an hour before you guys found me at the club. It turned into some whole big thing and ended with her walking out."

"Dammit." She wraps her arms around her thin body to protect against the cold air, but she doesn't go back inside. She must really care.

"It's over. I have to resign myself to that."

"No! You can't give up that easily."

"Chloe, you don't know. Okay? You just don't." My voice gets sharp.

"What don't I know?" she shouts over the noise of the traffic going up and down the street.

"You don't know how she looked. I broke her heart. I didn't mean to, I swear to God. I wouldn't hurt her for anything in the world, but I did because I'm a selfish bastard." I'm surprised to feel my eyes burning. "I…I love her."

Her face softens. "Then you have to fight for her."

I shake my head even though this is eerily similar to what Jane said. That as soon as things were tough, I ran. Still... "It's a waste of time, Chloe. She made it pretty clear that she never wants to see me again."

"Anthony." She reaches out, putting a hand on my arm. "Did she tell you what happened to her when she was a kid?"

That sick feeling in my stomach comes rushing back, followed by the rage that made me track down that bastard uncle. I nod.

"That closed her off to men and relationships. She's been afraid ever since. Until now."

"Until me, you mean." I feel lower than dirt as I remember the trust she put in me...and then how I threw her past back in her face like a spoiled brat.

"Yes. Until you." Chloe looks me straight in the eye with the sort of no-nonsense stare that tells me she won't take any shit from me. "Which means if you really love her like you say you do, you have to fight for her. Prove that she can trust you."

I can't help but shake my head. "It's not that easy. This isn't the movies. What am I supposed to do?"

"Go to her, you idiot! Let her know that you choose her. Show her what she means to you. Don't just *tell* her. Do whatever you have to do for her to know that you're in this with her. That you'll do whatever it takes. She's too important to let slip through your fingers, Anthony."

"I know that," I snap. "You don't have to tell me."

"Apparently I do, or you'd already be on your way to her apartment." She spins on her heel and stalks back toward the door.

Damn.

I turn back to the car and know I have a decision to make. I can go home and lick my wounds, mope around like a little kid who hadn't gotten his way, or I can fight for the woman I love.

It's a no-brainer.

Twenty minutes later, I jump out of the car and run all the way up to Jane's apartment. I have to talk to her, face-to-face. I have to prove to her that her trust isn't misplaced. That I'm done running just because something is difficult. That I can be the man she deserves.

"Jane?" I'm practically banging the door down, but no one's answering.

"Hey!" I turn at the sound of a semi-hostile voice in

the hall. "What are you trying to do? Break in?" The woman is older, heavyset, and wears the sort of expression that tells me she doesn't take shit from anyone.

"Sorry, ma'am. I was looking for Jane."

"She left."

My heart drops. "Left? Like, left for good?"

"No." She rolls her eyes. "I mean left for an appointment or something. I was coming in with my groceries when she was leaving. She almost knocked me over when she ran past, down the hall. And she's usually such a polite girl."

I frown. "What was the hurry? Did she say?"

"Something about going to the office. An offer she couldn't refuse, I don't know." The woman waves a dismissive hand. "Like that makes up for being rude."

I absently thank the woman, but she's already closing her door. I'd been so ready to work things out that Jane's absence threw me for a loop. An offer she couldn't refuse. What's that supposed to mean?

CHAPTER TWENTY-EIGHT
JANE

On the list of things I thought would never happen, being called into the CEO's office after quitting has to rank right up near the top. Right up there with "sleeping with Anthony James," at least. Because I didn't see that one coming when I got this job.

I'm really batting a thousand lately.

What's even weirder, he called me personally—not personally as in through his assistant but actually himself—promising an offer I can't refuse. A little eye-rolling at the *Godfather* reference aside, I can't deny that he's piqued my interest. Does he even know I quit? Maybe he does and he's trying to offer me a better position in the company. Maybe he wants to apologize for his son being a total jackass. All right, that one's doubtful, but a girl can dream. Maybe I'd read him wrong and he really is a decent guy and Anthony is the jerk.

I sigh, because I know that's not the case.

My brain's still going a mile a minute as the elevator doors open. What if he tries to convince me to stay on with Anthony? What if Anthony went to his dad about what happened? I can just see it: Anthony whining to Daddy that he can't get what he wants, and Daddy swooping in to make things right. Probably to make himself look better, too. He wouldn't want a sexual harassment lawsuit on his hands, not that I would ever do something like that, but he doesn't know me. Powerful men like him have to be careful.

Marta smiles wide when she sees me approaching. "Jane, dear, I'm so glad to see you."

As if we didn't see each other yesterday. Still, I return her smile and keep my thoughts to myself as she leads me to the Big Man. It's not her fault Anthony and I fell apart.

Mr. James is standing when I walk inside, and the smile tells me immediately that something's up. He's trying to schmooze me. Unfortunately for him, with the one exception of his much more charismatic son, I'm not so easily charmed.

"Please, have a seat."

That entire politician persona is as strong as it was when we first met. I sit down in one of the chairs across from his desk, and he takes his seat. He folds his hands in front of him and his smile fades, replaced by a very serious expression. But it's still a false one, like he's trying to convince me that whatever he's going to say, he needs me to think that it's genuine.

"It's come to my attention that you were very poorly

used by my son."

I blink rapidly, trying to process that sentence. What's he talking about? He can't mean that he knows about Anthony and me, can he? "Excuse me?" I whisper.

"I understand that all the ideas presented to Chambersmith, Inc. were yours, not my son's."

I have a moment of relief when I realize that he's talking about business, but that quickly becomes confusion. How the hell can he possibly know that? Anthony wouldn't tell him, would he? No, he's a lot of things, but stupid's not one of them. I knew just as well as he did that we couldn't blab about our collaboration.

Not when he was so happy that his dad was proud of him.

Mr. James doesn't wait for me to reply. "You've shown a great deal of intelligence and savvy, Jane. The sort of qualities we want here at James Enterprises. When I found out you were the genius behind the campaign, I knew I had to have you as a full-time employee."

My eyes widen. It's just what Anthony promised when we first started working together, but this is coming from the CEO. I should be excited, but all I feel is a deep sense of dread that something else is coming.

"However," he adds, like it's an afterthought rather than a calculated move, "we would ask that you sign over all of your ideas retroactively. Just to keep everything on the up-and-up. You understand."

I finally notice the sheaf of papers sitting just to his right. A contract. And probably some sort of NDA. My head is spinning. Things are happening too fast.

I need to say something, and besides, curiosity is killing me. "What about Anthony?"

His expression slips just a bit, but he quickly recovers. "Anthony? What about him?"

His voice is stiff now, like my question caught him off guard.

I'm not going to back down, though. "I…I mean, where is he? What happened to him? You said you want me to sign over my ideas, but you didn't say anything about his. They were his ideas, too."

He scoffs, waving a dismissive hand. "He no longer works here. You don't have to worry about him."

What the hell does *that* mean?

"But—"

"You're very noble, trying to stand up for him the way you are. I can only imagine the way he sweet-talked his way into stealing those great ideas and letting him pass them off as his own." Cue mournful head shake. "He always does this, you know. Coasting by without doing any actual work. I'm sure he made you believe your ideas were his, too. It's shameful, really. I wish I knew where I went wrong with him."

My cheeks flush, and I hope he takes it as me being embarrassed rather than angry, because the way he's talking about Anthony is pissing me off. Okay, so maybe Anthony isn't everything I thought, but he doesn't deserve his father to talk about him that way.

I can't let it go.

"You know, sir, with all due respect, that work was just as much your son's as it was mine. The finished product, I mean. He took my ideas and made them better. He worked hard, probably harder than he ever has. We were a great team. I just thought you should know that." I can't believe I'm actually contradicting him, but it's not right for him to think so poorly of his own son.

He pauses for a second, and I wonder if he's taking me seriously.

No such luck.

"As I said, you don't have to worry about him anymore. Here." He slides the contract across the table as my heart sinks. It's like talking to a wall.

I turn my attention to what he's handed me. Not only is he offering me a salary with more zeroes than I've ever seen together at once, but he wants to pay me for my Chambersmith ideas. I know he's only covering his ass—I'm no idiot—but the thought that my ideas would pull down such a generous fee is gratifying. No, more than that. A dream come true.

So why don't I feel happy? The man is handing me everything I ever wanted. Real money. The chance to live in an apartment big enough for more than two people to be in at once. A life full of choices and opportunity.

Isn't that what I've always wanted?

"Well, Jane?" The bright smile is frozen on his face. "What do you say? Are you ready to start the rest of your life?" He holds a pen out to me.

Am I ready?

Good question.

CHAPTER TWENTY-NINE
JANE

Just when I think life can't surprise me any further, there's somebody waiting for me when I get home.

"What is this?" I linger by the stairs, wary at the sight of Anthony James sitting outside my apartment door. Anthony and several suitcases.

Okay, that's...curious.

He gets up, brushing off the seat of his jeans. Even in jeans he's delectable. I remind myself of how he broke my heart, and how much I hate him for it, before the sight of him melts my resolve like a dish of ice cream left out in the sun. His smile is genuine, but there's a little vulnerability in his eyes.

"This is me taking a stand for what I want, for once."

Well, that makes no sense. I wait for more, but that's as eloquent as he feels like being at the moment, apparently.

"Huh? And those are for...what? You think you're going to move in with me or something? Isn't that a bit of a step down for you? I don't even think all those suitcases could fit inside my place."

He laughs, and it's a real, honest sound. "Why don't you come a little closer, and I'll tell you why I'm really here? I don't feel like shouting down the hall for all your neighbors to hear."

Yes, but if I'm much closer to him, I won't be able to resist his charm. Damn him for always putting me in this position. Just once, I'd like to feel like I have the upper hand. I take one slow step after another until we're standing face-to-face, but on opposite sides of the hallway. I lean against the wall across from my door. That's as close as I trust myself to be to him.

"Okay. So? What's this all about?"

Instead of replying, he holds out one hand. But as I look down, I realize he's not trying to hold my hand. He's holding something out to me. Plane tickets. "I bought these for you and me."

I'm beginning to think that today is going to be all about blindsiding me.

"Excuse me?"

His voice is eager, hopeful. "I cashed in the last of my savings and bought these. They're open-ended. We can go anywhere you want. I don't care. As long as I'm with you, I'll be happy anywhere."

I bite down on my lip and try to process what he's telling me. I feel like I'm on overload. "You think I'll forget everything that's happened just because you throw a plane ticket at me? You think I can just drop my life and run off with you?"

To my surprise, he doesn't crack under my questions. He doesn't blow off what I'm feeling or saying. He doesn't tell me that it's too much. Instead, he says the last thing I expect.

"You're right. It's a lot to ask. But this is a gesture, more than anything else. Even if you don't want to go anywhere, that's fine. I'll stick around here. I'll give up everything—not that there's all that much to give up anymore. Nothing I care about anyway." He gives me a soft sort of smile, his eyes glowing. "You showed me that I had nothing before I met you. You're everything, and I meant it when I said I love you. That hasn't changed. I'll get a job, support you, whatever you want. As long as you're with me."

Less than an hour ago, someone offered me what I thought was everything. Now I see the truth, though. *This* is everything I've ever wanted. Not a job or money or a new apartment, but a man who loves me. A man who is willing to put his pride aside. To put aside everything else. For me.

It's all so clear now.

He's so hopeful as he waits for me to respond. His eyes radiate love and hope. He wants *me*. *Us*. He's willing to throw away everything to be with me. He's choosing me even though he knows it's going to be hard.

After a long, silent moment, I finally give him a response. "You don't have to do any of that—supporting me, I mean."

The light leaves his eyes, and his shoulders slump. "You're saying no?"

I shake my head. "I'm saying I don't need the money. Your father offered me a job."

He takes it surprisingly well. "I should've known. Well, congratulations. You deserve it."

"I didn't take it."

The light reappears. "You didn't?"

I shake my head with a smile. "Not after what he said about you. I could never work for him, knowing the kind of person he is. Let him work with your cousin and be around a suck-up all day long. They deserve each other."

His laugh is music to my ears. "I can't believe it! Somebody finally said no to my old man. He's probably still trying to process it."

I can't help but laugh with him. "Yeah, he did seem a little taken aback. I did say yes to one thing, though. The offer to pay me for the Chambersmith ideas in exchange for an NDA about my part in it." I take a dramatic pause as my smile widens. I can hardly believe it, but my name's right there on the check. "A quarter of a million dollars, in fact."

He beams, and all I see is pride on his face. Not a trace of jealousy or resentment. "You deserve it. I'm so happy for you."

When he opens his arms to me, I walk into them. I don't even have to think about it.

"I'm so sorry for everything," he whispers in my ear as I sink into his embrace. "You were right. I should have been honest with you. And I've always ran when things get hard, but not anymore."

"I'm sorry, too," I say. "We both should've been honest. Let's promise to do better from here on out."

"You deserve better than me, Jane, but I swear I'll do everything in my power to earn your trust back."

I pull away to look up into his eyes. "I believe you. And I trust you."

"I meant it when I said I love you. I love you so much, Jane." He runs his fingertips over my cheek, then along my jawline until he reaches my chin. His touch is soft and electric and everything.

He's everything.

"I love you, too." There are tears in my eyes when he pulls me closer for the deepest, sweetest kiss of my life.

The first of what I hope will be many.

CHAPTER THIRTY

JANE

“Yes, we would love the opportunity to work with you. We’re flattered you’re willing to give us a chance. I’m sure you’ll find out first-hand that we deliver on our promises,” Anthony says, giving me a silent high-five as he continues to close our latest account.

I turn back to my laptop with a smile. It looks like we’re about to add another name to our growing client list.

In moments like this one, with the man I love sitting behind me and the entire world stretching out in front of me outside the window, I’m almost sure I must be dreaming. It doesn’t seem possible that this is my life.

I can’t help but stare out the window above my desk over and over throughout the day. In fact, some of my best ideas crop up when I’m gazing at the wide, vast fields just beyond the little house that’s been our home for the last eight months.

Not just our home, either. Our office. The headquarters of the advertising world’s newest sensation—

at least, that's how we see it. Who needs a big, fancy office in the middle of Manhattan? It's a virtual world nowadays. Besides, we can visit our clients in the city. We're less than an hour away. Of course, those miles make all the difference in the world. I belong here, and once Anthony got used to it, he decided he did, too. His reaction the first time he caught an opossum going through our garbage still makes me giggle whenever I think about it, even though I do my best not to let him see. He could take a bourbon bottle to the head, but the sight of a little animal made him turn white as a ghost. I was fairly sure he might pass out.

The city never suited me. Sure, it was fun living there for a little while, but it didn't take long for me to understand that I loved the idea of it much more than the reality. I'm a country girl at heart—always will be. Anthony finally acknowledged that most of his trouble came from being in the city. He decided it would do him good to live more simply. Besides, he did say he would follow me wherever I wanted to go. Once I had the money, the man, and the opportunity to make a change, it was a no-brainer.

Now, I love waking up in the morning and enjoying a cup of coffee on the front porch while the sun rises. There's nothing like that beautiful peace before the world has woken up. I didn't understand quite how much I missed it before I got back to it. And now I'm here on my own terms, not anyone else's. We chose a new place rather than going back to PA, so we both are starting new. Neither of us are defined by who our parents were or are. We are ourselves, and only who we want to be.

And I love it. Nothing beats the joy of sitting back-to-back in our office, listening to him doing business. He knows his stuff. Once he no longer had to put up with his father, he discovered how truly good he is at advertising. He always jokes he must've learned by osmosis or something, but I know he's only downplaying his talent and intelligence. Nobody ever gave him credit for that before. Now he can shine out of his dad's shadow.

"That sounds fantastic. We'll have a rough outline to you by the end of the week." I swivel around in my chair in time to see the satisfied smile on his face, and my heart soars.

"So?" I ask.

"So, it looks like yet another of James Enterprises' top clients is looking for new, more modern representation." He leans back, grinning from ear to ear. "Nobody would believe it if we told them these people are coming to us, not the other way around."

"Especially your father."

"Especially him." He shrugs. "He's afraid of change. He won't even let his employees work remotely."

Meanwhile, we've just hired our first employee, a girl who lives halfway across the country. She'll be managing our calendars along with other administrative tasks. It'll free us up to do more of the creative work, which we both prefer. If we keep growing at the pace we've set—we already have six clients, three of whom were James Enterprises clients who jumped ship when they heard what we cooked up for Chambersmith—we'll need to start building a creative team. We both wish we could've kept that account, but I already signed the campaign over. Maybe somewhere down the line, when they're looking for a change, they'll come back to us.

"A new client," Anthony says. "I think this calls for a celebration."

My pulse picks up speed, and I feel warm all over. "Oh? What do you have in mind?"

"I think you know what I have in mind." His wicked grin is just about the sexiest thing I've ever seen. When he stands and comes to me, all I can see is him.

He cups my face as he takes my lips, his tongue tangling with mine as it plunges into my mouth. I grab the waist of his jeans, and he bites down on my bottom lip, urging me onward. He's half-hard as I wrap my fingers around him, and I begin to stroke him. His hands go to my shirt, pulling at the neck of my tank top until both of my breasts are exposed.

He pinches and tugs at my nipples until I moan into his mouth. He lifts me out of the chair, and I break the kiss to rid me of my pants. He curses when he sees that I'm not wearing panties. I like to do that once or twice a week, just to keep things interesting. Sort of like how he likes to take me in all sorts of different locations.

In the field under the stars.

Every single room in our house, including the pantry.

At the nearest town's drive-in.

Today, it's in my office chair.

He grabs my waist and lifts me, turning us both

before sitting down. I rest on my knees, straddling his lap. His mouth latches on to my breasts as I sink down onto his hard shaft. We did away with condoms six months back, but I still marvel at the feel of skin against skin.

We move together faster, knowing this will be only the first of several times we'll come together over the next few hours. I bury my fingers in his hair, holding his head to my chest. He's rough with my nipples, but all it does is make me slam down on him hard enough to make stars spark in front of my eyes.

His hips jerk under me, and I yank his head back so that our eyes meet as we come together. I feel him pulse inside me, filling me, and I smile at the knowledge that someday, in the near future, I'll put aside my birth control and this act of love will be the beginning of the family that the two of us have always wanted.

He's looking at me with those dark, smoldering eyes of his, and I know we're just getting started.

Later, in bed together and considerably sweatier than we were in our little home office, I lift my head from his chest to ask, "Will it always be this way?"

I know he knows what I'm asking. Will we always be this happy? Will I always feel a rush of bliss when he kisses me? Or when our eyes meet from across the dining room table, or when he does something as simple as taking my hand while we're out for a walk? Will we always work so well together? Will we always work hard to make our dreams real?

His smile is warm, sure, loving. Everything I've ever wanted, from the sort of man I've always wanted. "I can't imagine life any other way," he promises. He kisses my cheek, then frowns. "What's wrong?"

"I have a secret," I say sheepishly. "It's the last one, I promise."

"Okay, what is it?"

"That night we..." My cheeks flush and this time it's from embarrassment rather than arousal. "It was my first time."

He still looks confused.

"I'm a virgin," I blurt out, then immediately correct myself. "I was, I mean, before you."

He smiles and kisses my forehead. "And I was a player before I met you. Good thing we met, or we'd both still be doomed."

"So you're not mad I didn't tell you?" I ask.

He shakes his head. "Why would I be mad? You just told me that I'm the only person who knows what it's like to see you come, to know what it's like to be inside you."

A wave of relief washes over me, and I brush my lips across his. "I love you."

"I love you, too." His eyes twinkle. "Now, what do you say we make sure that virginity's really gone? I wouldn't want to let you down."

I smile up at him as he rolls me underneath him. "Not a chance of that."

SNEAK PEEK
VIP:TAKEN BY THE BILLIONAIRE
CHAPTER ONE

DANIELA

Another day, another dollar.

That's what I tell myself as I clean a glass and place it carefully underneath the bar at Trinity, a local dive in Chicago. I wash another one, doing my best to ignore the creep who continues to edge toward me from his side of the bar.

"Hey, baby, come on," he says, cocking his head, his hands straying closer to me. "When do you finish your shift? We could get a drink."

"I'm good," I respond calmly, but I'm starting to get pissed. He's been at this for the last half hour, and since I'm the only bartender on duty right now, I'm an easy target. At this time of day, there's only a handful of other people scattered around the room. The odd couple having a conversation in hushed tones next to the window, and a woman drinking alone at the other end of the bar.

"What can I do to convince you?" he whines, sounding like a toddler denied his favorite toy.

Okay, now I'm getting seriously pissed.

I slam down the wine glass I'm cleaning on the bar between us. "I'm not interested. Okay, buddy?" I lower my eyebrows, giving him my best glower. "Either cut it out or go to another bar."

Of course, the universe immediately punishes me for standing up for myself.

As soon as the words are out of my mouth, he raises his hands in a defensive gesture and knocks the glass off the edge of the bar. Even as I reach for it, I know that I should just let it smash, clean it up, and use it as an excuse to kick his ass out. But instead, on instinct, I try to catch it. As I lunge forward, it hits one of the shelves beneath the bar, cracks into several pieces, and a large fragment spins off, landing a deep cut between my thumb and forefinger.

"Motherfucker!" I yell, too annoyed with myself to register the pain as blood begins to drip steadily from the gash in my hand. My eyes shoot up, and the guy's face goes white. He quickly looks away, pretending he doesn't see the chaos he created.

"Asshole," I mutter to myself as I grab a towel and head toward the employee bathroom to clean up.

As I run the water, I'm so focused on my hand that I barely notice Tina enter the room. She must have just gotten in to join me for the evening rush. She's been mixing drinks here at Trinity Sports Bar for as long as I've known her and is actually the one who recommended me to the manager.

"Shit, Daniela!" She takes my wrist and pulls it towards her. "What happened?"

"Nothing," I mumble, but she's already leading me through to the staffroom.

"I'm getting you bandaged up," she says firmly and reaches for the first aid kit. I feel my head start to swim as I watch her try to fix me up. The blood doesn't seem to want to stop.

"What's going on in here?" Dennis, the manager, appears at the door. He sounds even more pissed off than usual.

"Uh, there was a guest out there." I nod toward the bar. "He was hassling me, and–"

"He says you went crazy on him." Dennis raises his eyebrows and crosses his arms. "Says you threw a glass at his head."

"Jesus Christ, Dennis. Can't you see how badly hurt she is?" Tina snaps. Dennis shoots her a look, and she quiets down. She needs this job as much as the rest of us, no matter how much of an asshole our boss is.

"Is that true? Did you throw a glass at him? Is that how you got that cut?"

"Bullshit!" An unfamiliar voice enters the equation. "That's so not what happened."

We all turn, and Dennis steps aside to reveal the only other woman in the bar standing behind him. She's taller than she looked sitting down.

"I saw everything," she continues. "That asshole was the one who shoved the glass off the counter. She went to catch it, and that's when she got hurt."

She shoots me a conciliatory look, and I nod back with a grateful smile. With only a few words, my ass is officially saved.

The woman steps into the room. "He's really drunk. I don't even think he should be in here, but yeah...it was totally that guy's fault."

"Thanks for your help." Dennis plasters on his prime customer-pleasing grin. He turns to me with a rare look of apology on his face. "I'll get him chucked out," he mumbles and then gestures to my hand. "You should get that looked at. Take the rest of the day off."

ꕥ

After the nurse practitioner at the urgent care center dumped a glob of what looked like superglue in my cut and steri-stripped it together, I'm on my way with a warning to keep the wound dry for a couple of days and watch out for signs of infection. A nice tetanus shot rounds out the visit, and I know I'll feel that muscle for a while.

"Thanks, Mom," I mutter, feeling petulant and childish, but unable to help myself. I love my mom, but she checked out of this world a couple years ago, overtaken by bouts of depression so deep she's been hospitalized several times. I have great sympathy for her illness, but sometimes, I just need my mother to answer the phone. I miss talking to her and asking things as simple as when my last vaccinations were.

Guilt immediately follows these negative thoughts, and I cross the street, heading to the nursing home located down the block. Outside its doors, I take a deep breath and plaster a smile on my face.

"Hi, Judy," I say to the receptionist as I sign in.

The older lady gives me a motherly grin. "Hi, Daniela. You're here awfully early today."

I hold up my bandaged hand, and her smile fades away. "It's no big deal. Just got me out of work earlier than usual."

She gives me the same *watch out for infection* lecture I'd just endured, then buzzes me through the security door. I walk the familiar hallway, then bounce up the stairs until I'm on the third-floor residence hall. Here, the living accommodations are more like apartments and couples can live together in the space with minimal assistance from the staff. When we moved to Chicago a couple years ago, finding this place was like a miracle for both of my parents.

Outside of their room, I take another deep breath and gently push open the door. Mom is lying on her bed, curled up in a tight ball while Dad watches TV from his, the dialysis machine churning its blood cleansing wheels beside him.

"Hey, Dani-bean," Dad calls out when he sees me. I frown at how pale he is. I plaster on the smile again and walk over to his bed. He clicks off the television and pats the mattress for me to take a seat next to him. I do and am soon enfolded next to his warmth – the safest place I've ever known.

"How are you feeling?" I ask him after a few minutes, but already know what his answer will be.

"Fine and dandy," we say together and laugh. It's the same response I get every day.

Diagnosed as a teenager with what was then called juvenile diabetes, his disease has been progressively working on his kidneys until it became clear that a transplant was his only option. I hug him tighter, willing his name to miraculously jump up higher on the donor list before his body is too weak for the operation. Normal wait time is four to six years, and he's already been on the list for nearly three.

I stay until he grows tired, then kiss him on the forehead and say my goodbyes. I step over to Mom's bed and give her a kiss too, wishing there was an operation that could fix the progressive deterioration of her mind and spirit.

Minutes later, I'm sitting in a cab on the way back to my apartment. Well, *our* apartment – it still feels weird to think of it that way. Pete and I have been dating almost two years and have lived together for one. We met at a club where he was DJing. I was tending the bar and we bumped into each other when we both headed outside for a break. The rest is history.

Before we met, I was living in a cramped apartment with three roommates, so moving in with him saved my sanity. I look at my watch and smile. Pete should still be home, and I could use a little sanity saving right now.

Pete is a self-diagnosed sex addict, and he never stops going at it. If I just hint that I'm in the mood, he'll be rubbing up on me in a nanosecond. Even though he's twenty-four now, he still has the libido of a fifteen-year-old who's just seen his first pair of tits.

I squirm in my seat just thinking about being with him. He's by far the hottest guy I've ever slept with, although that's not saying much. There wasn't exactly a wide choice of sex gods back in my little hometown of Pella, Iowa. So when Pete entered my life, all muscles and cropped hair and cheekbones, I felt as though I'd hit some crazy lottery. Yeah, he's not the smartest, and he flirts too much with other women, but hey, with that body and face, I can't complain.

I'm ready for something wild…maybe anal? Pete always asks, but we've never actually done it because I'm nervous it might hurt. But today, a little pain, followed by a delightful orgasm, might just be what the doctor ordered to make me forget this entire day. I run my fingers through my hair and pull out my phone, inspecting myself using the selfie camera. I look a mess, but a dab of makeup will cover up the worst.

I pay the driver and hop out of the cab, fumbling awkwardly with my opposite hand in my pocket to find my keys. I unlock the door and sashay my way up the stairs, doing my best to feel sexy as I open the door to the apartment. That's when I hear it.

The unmistakable sound of sex coming from our bedroom.

Bedsprings are creaking rhythmically, and Pete's small

moans of pleasure echo throughout the house. I close the door quietly, not sure how to react, and make my way across the hall. I press my ear to the bedroom door, and I could swear that…

Before I can finish my thought, the door flies open, and I tumble into the room. I gape at the display before me. Pete is standing in front of me, stark naked, and in our bed is a…*guy*. The covers are pulled haphazardly around him so I can't see if he's naked too, but I'm not stupid enough to place money against that one.

My face feels numb as all the blood drains into my toes. I open my mouth to say something–

"I'm sorry," he blurts out before I can utter a sound. "I thought you were at work."

"S-so?" I manage to say, clutching my hand, which has started to emit a low dull throbbing in rhythm to my pounding heart.

"So…" He gestures to the guy behind him. "I know I should have told you sooner–"

I begin to snap back into reality. "Wait, how long has this been going on?"

"Uh, a couple weeks?" Pete flashes me a smile as if I'm just going to roll over and take this.

"And is he the first…?" I trail off, not sure whether I should specify gender. I'm too shell-shocked to really know what I need to find out.

"Uh, yeah," Pete runs a hand through his hair, and I can see that he's lying.

"Hey, you want to join us or not?" The guy in the bed props up on his elbows and raises his eyebrows at me.

My mouth opens in disbelief, but nothing comes out. Again, I'm speechless.

Pete scratches the stubble on his chin. "Could be fun."

"Fuck you!" I snap, finding my anger at last. "I'm leaving."

"When will you be back?" Pete asks casually as if this is nothing more than a mild disagreement.

"I won't," I snarl. "We're done."

"Dani, wait!" he calls as I storm out of the room. I ignore him and slam the door so hard I hear the bed shake. I'll come back later to pick up my stuff, but right now, I need to get the hell away from here.

I make it down to the street before it hits me. Just like that, I'm single again. And homeless. I don't cry, which surprises me. After my last breakup, I bawled my eyes out for a full week, and we'd only been together six months. I guess somewhere in the back of my mind, I always suspected that Pete wasn't entirely faithful, but his bisexuality, well, that was a surprise.

It's a hot and humid Chicago day, and the sweat is pouring off me as I walk fast, barely noticing my surroundings. I'm trying to put as much space as I possibly can between my cheating ex-boyfriend and me.

I look up and realize that I'm outside of work. The faded Trinity Bar sign sits a few feet over my head, and I sigh when I think about what this says about me. My safe place is my job? That's shitty. Since I'm here, I might as well find out if I can make up the hours I missed earlier. My hand feels better, and I could sure use the extra tips.

Inside, it's even more humid than on the streets. The crowds are gathering for the Friday night drinking marathon. I squeeze through the reams of people, exchanging a few loaded looks with a couple of cute guys who give me the up and down. I can't imagine I'm looking my best, but I appreciate the attention.

Dennis has left, replaced by Sheila, the night manager.

Everyone prefers her to the asshole because she's a lot easier to get along with.

"Hey, Sheila." I stick my head into her office, and she jolts slightly at my appearance.

"Surprised to see you here," she says and leans back in her seat. "Dennis told me you had a pretty nasty accident earlier today. He sent you to the ER, right?"

"Yeah." I fight the urge to roll my eyes at the mere mention of Dennis's name. "But I'm all put together again, and I've got the evening off, so I thought–?"

"If you think I'm going to let you out there on a Friday night with your hand sliced and diced, you've got another thing coming." Sheila gets to her feet and steps toward me. "Come on. Go home, get some rest. Get that cute and sexy boyfriend of yours to look after you."

I try to hide the look of disappointment on my face. "Sure," I mumble, not ready to share the news of our break-up with anyone. I sidle back into the bar, scanning the place. Time to change my luck. I've had a creep coming on to me, an accident that sent me to the emergency room, and a break-up with my boyfriend of two years, all in one day. As my old daddy always says – *when life hands you lemons, make whiskey sour.*

I push my way through to the bar and lean on the counter, catching Tina's eye. She quickly heads my way and deftly pours a shot into a small glass, shoving it toward me.

"This will help. How's your hand?" She frowns sympathetically.

"They just dumped some of that glue stuff in it. It's nothing, really." I offer her my best fake smile and reach for the drink with my bad hand – wincing. I withdraw it and use the other to toss back the shot.

"Be careful. You'll tear it open. I've got to serve that

group over there," Tina nods to a table at the other side of the bar, "but I'll catch you soon, yeah?"

"Sure thing."

I watch her leave and fight the urge to reach over the bar and pour myself another shot. One thing is certain, after this long fucked-upped day, all I want to do is get wasted.

"Are you okay?"

I jump as a soft hand lands on my shoulder. I turn and see the woman who defended me earlier. I give her a smile. "Yeah, thanks. I really appreciate you stepping up for me."

She holds out a hand. "I'm Aria," she says as she takes a seat beside me.

I'm grateful that my wound is on my left hand as we shake. "Daniela."

"Are you sure you're okay," she asks, eyeing me closely. "You seem…upset."

I'm not sure why, but I feel tears prick the back of my eyes. I blink hard, willing them away.

Aria squeezes my fingers. "Oh, honey, want to talk about it?"

I look into her eyes and realize I do. Maybe talking to a stranger will be easier than with a friend.

As I spill my story, Aria orders us both a straight whiskey.

"I didn't even know he was bi," I complain and take a sip.

She winks at me. "Nothing wrong with that," she says with a laugh.

I laugh too and the stress of the day seems to float away. Maybe it's the effects of the whiskey, but I think it's more that I'm able to get all this burden off my chest.

"Thanks for listening to all that," I tell her and raise my glass in a silent toast.

She clinks her glass to mine. "Anytime. And speaking of anytime, how about this weekend?"

I look at her curiously. "What do you mean?"

She leans closer. "My aunt has this amazing house down in Fort Lauderdale, Florida. I'm heading down there this weekend for a party but I hate traveling alone. You should come with me. Plenty of hot and sexy guys. Nothing like getting your mind off a guy than a quick fling with another guy."

I smile. "That sounds incredible, but right now, I can't even afford a McDonalds happy meal, much less a plane ticket."

"Oh, honey." Aria laughs. "You'll be so glad you met me. I've got like two million flying miles saved up. We'll get you a ticket."

I look up from the amber liquid I'd been staring at and meet Aria's eyes. "Seriously?"

Aria nods. "Seriously."

It's tempting. Florida does sound better than Chicago any day of the week.

"Come on," Aria says as I hesitate. "The ocean. Hot guys. Free getaway with a new friend. How can you say no to all that?"

How indeed?

About Tasha

I'm originally from a small southern town where everyone knew everyone and their business. I was so happy to leave and move to California for college where I was originally going to be a veterinarian.

Well, I met a guy – yeah, it's that kind of story – and dropped out of school to have my oldest daughter. We soon divorced, and as a kind of therapy, I started to write books. I loved the fantasy world of fiction and never did go back to college, and have been writing ever since.

I write about sexy guys and girls. Anything but missionary – unless the heroine is tied up tight. My southern upbringing sure brings the kinkiness out of me. Don't be shy to stay in touch. I'd love to hear your kinky stories. Maybe we can turn them into a book. :)

XXX, Tasha

Please visit me at and get a free ebook!
http://tashafawkes.com/

Copyright

Published by: Safira Publishing

Made in the USA
San Bernardino, CA
23 July 2018